SOLOMON'S TALE

Sheila Jeffries has been writing since she was young, and penned four children's novels which were published before she left school. Written under her maiden name, Sheila Chapman, in the popular 'pony story' genre of the time, the books continued to sell worldwide until the eighties.

After studying at Bath Academy of Art, Sheila spent many happy years teaching in UK schools. She had eight more children's novels published under the name Sheila Haigh, and her most successful book, *Little Gymnast*, was a best seller in America.

Solomon's Tale breaks new ground in her writing career. It's a book truly from the heart, and though it is fiction it is based on two real cats, Solomon and Jessica, who shared and enriched her life.

Sheila lives in Somerset where she enjoys teaching meditation and running workshops for writers.

D1428784

SOLOMON'S Tale

SHEILA JEFFRIES

AVON

AVON

A division of HarperCollins*Publishers*
77–85 Fulham Palace Road,
London W6 8JB

www.harpercollins.co.uk

A Paperback Original 2014
1

Copyright © Sheila Jeffries 2013

Sheila Jeffries asserts the moral right to
be identified as the author of this work

A catalogue record for this book is
available from the British Library

ISBN 978-0-00-755766-0

Set in Bembo by Ben Gardiner

Printed and bound in Great Britain by Clays Ltd, St Ives plc

A warm thank you to my husband, Ted, my agent, Judith Murdoch, my editor, Helen Bolton, and to Solomon who really was my lucky black cat.

To Andrea, Annette, Val, Jackie and Pauline

CONTENTS

Chapter One
Finding Ellen

Chapter Two
Another Cat Got There First

Chapter Three
The Bailiff

Chapter Four
Leaving Home

Chapter Five
That Dog

Chapter Six
Going to the Vet

Chapter Seven
'You Cheeky Cat'

Chapter Eight
The Marmite Sandwich

Chapter Nine
Abandoned

Chapter Ten
The Diary of a Desperate Cat

Chapter Eleven
If Cats Could Cry

Chapter Twelve
The Diary of a Star Cat

A Note on Tuxedo Cats
The Real Life Solomon
The Orphaned Kittens

SOLOMON'S
Tale

CHAPTER ONE

FINDING ELLEN

I sat down in the middle of the road to think about why I had left home on that summer morning.

I was only a black kitten, eight weeks old, but I had a tough decision to make. Should I stay in my comfortable home and live a boring predictable life, or should I set out on a long journey to find the person I loved best in the whole world? Her name was Ellen, and I had been Ellen's cat in another lifetime, when she was a child. She'd called me Solomon and I was her best friend. I wanted to find her again.

Suddenly a lorry was coming towards me. The road underneath my paws started to tremble. I could feel it vibrating along my tail and tickling the fluff inside my ears.

It loomed closer. Two glaring eyes, a forehead made of glass, and a name emblazoned across its chin. SCANIA. It had massive wheels and was roaring like fifty lions.

Hypnotised, I stared into its eyes, thinking that if I acted like an assertive tiger, the lorry would stop and let me finish washing my paws.

My angel didn't usually shout at me, but she did now. 'Run Solomon. RUN!'

I took off so fast that I left skid marks in the gravel. As I sailed into the hedge, the lorry thundered past in a gale of gritty air. Hissing, it pulled over, stopped, and was finally silent. A man climbed out and disappeared into a nearby building.

Being a very nosy kitten, I crept out to inspect the giant lorry while it was quiet. I sat in the road and looked at it. The sky darkened and icy hailstones came pinging down into my fur. Underneath the lorry was a good place to shelter. The wheels were hot and I sat close to one, watching the hailstones bouncing on the tarmac. I'd been outside for a long time and I needed to sleep.

I crawled into a hole at the front of the lorry. Inside, it was toasty warm. The stink of oil, the heat, and the chorus of hailstones made me drowsy. I curled up on a little shelf close to the engine, wrapped my tail around the tip of my nose, and fell asleep.

Hours later, I was jolted awake by an ear-splitting clatter. Every bone in my body was being banged up and down as the engine hammered into life. Terrified, I scrabbled to get out but saw only a chink of speeding wet road. I climbed higher, onto an oily ledge, my white-tipped paws ruined and stinking. Through a crack in the metal was a view of fields and bridges racing past.

I clung there, trying to communicate with my angel. But all she said was, 'your journey has begun, Solomon'.

I understood.

And I remembered how, before I was even born, I had agreed to make the perilous journey to find Ellen.

It all began when I was a shining cat, living in the spirit world between lifetimes.

In the spirit world we cats are shining cats, and we live in a way that is impossible on earth. We are invisible to human eyes. There is no meowing or yowling, but we do purr, and we communicate by telepathy. Lots of other creatures live there, shining dogs and shining horses, even shining guinea pigs. There are shining people too. No one argues. There is no pollution, no illness, and no war.

Ellen's mum had died when Ellen was young, and now she lived in the spirit world with me. She knew how much Ellen missed her and it was her idea to send me.

'I'd like to send Ellen a cat,' she said, 'a special cat to love and support her. She's going to need it with that husband of hers.'

My response was immediate.

'I'll go.'

Ellen's mum took me onto her lap, where I did lots of purring, and together we sent the idea out into the light. Then we waited until an angel appeared.

Thousands of angels live in the spirit world, and they are all different. Some of them are immense and glittering warriors of light. Others change colour like holograms. My favourite ones are the comfort angels who are more like people, and their robes are soft and swishy. They shine so brightly that their faces are almost invisible.

The angel who came to us introduced herself as the Angel of the Silver Stars. I'd never seen her before, but as soon as her twinkling robe billowed around me I felt special.

'I'll be your angel for this lifetime, Solomon,' she said. 'It will be a tough assignment, but I will be there to advise you about the choices you make. Of course you will make mistakes, but that is part of your learning, and I will still be there for you. My light is so bright that I become almost invisible on earth, but if you remember to look at sparkles whenever you can, you will see me, especially if you study the sunlight glittering on water.'

'I'll remember,' I said, and hoped that I would.

'There will be times when you are upset or lost or hungry,' said my angel as she covered me in stardust. 'That's when you might forget me, but I'll be there, and from time to time other angels will come to help the humans in your life. But don't expect it to be easy.'

It didn't sound difficult to me, since I already loved Ellen. My mind was buzzing with excitement at the prospect of going to earth again. There would be tins of Kitekat, and cosy fires, and all those mice. I couldn't wait.

'You'll have to be born as a kitten in the usual way,' said the Angel of the Silver Stars. 'I'll help you, but you must help yourself too. It's not just about Ellen. You've still got stuff to learn.'

'I'd like to be a majestic tomcat,' I said, 'with a really powerful purr. Black and glossy, with white paws and a white chest. And please will you send me to the right address? Last time it involved being dumped at the RSPCA before Ellen found me.'

'This time you will have to find her,' said the angel. 'You must learn to use your psi sense.'

'Psi sense?' I asked.

'Humans call it Sat Nav,' said the angel with a smile. 'Are you sure you want to go, Solomon?'

Nostalgically I gazed around at my beautiful home in the spirit world. I loved being a shining cat. Here, you could just *be*. No one would chuck you out in the rain, or cover you in flea powder.

Then I remembered Ellen's house, with its sunny windows. My favourite cushion was there, made of amber velvet. And the stairs were my best ever playground. Ellen had a cosy kitchen and a cherry tree in the garden.

I'd been Ellen's cat when she was a child, and she'd loved me more than anyone else in her life. She wouldn't go to sleep unless I was there, purring on her bed, and when her mum had turned out the light and gone downstairs, Ellen would turn it on again and play with me. When we were tired, Ellen showed me her secret diary, and read it to me. She had a lovely musical voice, and I was the only one who heard it because Ellen wouldn't talk to people very much. She wouldn't do her homework or tidy her bedroom. All she wanted to do was dance, and play the piano.

The best memory I had of Ellen was the way she shared her musical gifts with me. Early in the morning she sat down at the piano, on the velvet stool, and she was so small that her feet didn't reach the floor.

'Come on, Solomon,' she'd say, and smile as I jumped up to lie on top of the shiny piano. I liked to be there and see the light in her eyes as she played, and watch her come to life. She played on and on, with her tiny hands dancing over the keys, her blonde hair bouncing. The music gave me a buzz, up my spine and along my whiskers. At those times there were always angels shimmering around us.

Her mum would come in with Ellen's school bag and coat over her arm. 'It's time for school.'

'I don't want to go there, Mummy.'

'You're going.'

'But I want to finish playing this tune, Mummy. I made it up and Solomon loves it.'

'Ellen, it's TIME FOR SCHOOL.'

I had to watch helplessly as the light drained away from Ellen. Her small face tightened, her skin paled and her eyes clouded as she closed the lid of the piano.

'Listen to me, Solomon,' my angel said, and I focused on her again.

'Ellen is grown up now. She's not the child you remember.'

'So what's the problem?' I asked.

'I must warn you that Ellen is in such a state that she may not be able to look after you properly,' said my angel. 'She has a little boy who is just toddling, and a husband who shouts at her, and they are in desperate trouble.'

'I want to go,' I said firmly.

My angel hesitated, as if she wanted to tell me something else.

'And,' she whispered, 'there's Jessica.'

'Jessica?'

My angel was silent. She looked at me lovingly with her silver eyes.

'I'm sure Solomon will be fine,' said Ellen's mum. 'He's a healing cat. And he's brave and cheeky too. He'll be OK.'

When the time came for me to be born, I watched my angel dissolve into a kaleidoscope of sparks. The silver stars turned hazy, and suddenly I was whizzing through space. The light crackled like fire, and I burst through the great golden web which separates the spirit world from the earth. It was a brilliant ride.

Then everything changed.

I was no longer a shining spirit cat. I had to be compacted to fit inside this tiny sausage of a kitten, which had just been born. All I could do was wriggle and squeak. My eyes wouldn't open. My legs wouldn't walk. I couldn't see what colour my fur was. It was devastating. Why did I agree to do this? I wasn't a proper cat. I was a sausage.

But I wasn't alone. Four of us lay there in a purring heap, all silky and rhythmic. The power of the mother cat enveloped my whole being as she licked and suckled me.

Nine days later, my eyes opened to see the edge of a basket close to a warm stove. I saw my paws and they were glossy black with white toes, just as I'd requested. Big feet were walking around, two in slippers and two in boots, and hands kept coming down to gently stroke our tiny heads. It wasn't Ellen, but I kept faith that she would come and choose me.

My early kittenhood was happy. Right from the start I was picked up and held tenderly against massive chests, with hearts beating so slowly I thought those humans would die between beats.

'He'll be the last to go, that little black one with the white paws. They always choose the pretty ones first.'

'Yes well he's the runt of the litter. He's so small.'

The runt of the litter! Me?! That couldn't be true.

Soon we had turned into proper little cats, bouncing like tennis balls, climbing up curtains and under chair covers, with the humans laughing at us. But I was impatient to grow up and get to Ellen.

'He's got a wistful look, that little black one.'

Looking out of the window was my obsession, waiting for Ellen to come down the road. People began to arrive to choose kittens, and each time my whiskers stiffened to attention.

'Hide!' said my angel sharply one afternoon. It was the first time she had spoken to me since my birth, so my reaction was fast. Through a hole in the fabric, I shot into the dusty innards of the armchair to listen to the latest arrivals.

'I would have loved a black one.'

It wasn't Ellen's voice.

'We have got a black one somewhere.'

'Try under the chair.'

They slid the chair back, with me clinging well concealed inside, but they didn't find me.

Finally the visitors took both the remaining kittens, and when I emerged there was no one to play with. I was eight weeks old, and about to grow up in a hurry.

Ellen didn't come. Days and weeks went by and still there was no sign of her.

I stopped eating. Food was of no interest to a cat with a mission. The window was the only place to be, watching for Ellen.

'He's sick.'

'Take him to the vet.'

They did, and that was my first experience of the cat basket, a terrible cage that squeaks and bounces you up and down. Being a wise cat, I sat quietly, thinking how pointless it would be to waste my energy trying to escape.

The vet held me firmly by the scruff while he ran his thumbs over my body. He squeezed my paws and all along my tail. Then he forced my mouth open to look inside. I noticed his fingers smelled like the kitchen floor. He put me down on a cold table and said something very insulting to a proud young cat like me.

'Of course he's the runt of the litter.'

'But he's very loving. He's got a really special personality. If no one chooses him, we're going to keep him.'

My mum cat bullied me into eating, but still I pined for Ellen. Exploring the garden and seeking out high places to sit and watch for her became my favourite pastime.

Seeing my angel was more difficult now that I was in a body. To see my angel on earth I had to concentrate on ignoring everything else, but even then it was disappointing to see her so mistily.

'It's no good just waiting, Solomon,' she said. 'Use your psi sense.'

Midsummer morning was overcast and dark. I closed my eyes and used what the angel had called my psi sense. Immediately Ellen's location was obvious. She was due south of here, and it was surprisingly easy for me to sense the direction. The distance came more slowly, chilling me with the realisation that Ellen's house was hundreds of miles away. I looked at my delicate white-tipped paws and twitched my long whiskers. A hundred-mile journey was some challenge for the runt of the litter. That description stirred up enough anger to fire me into action. Without a backward glance I trotted down the road, to the south.

And that is how I ended up inside the engine of a lorry.

I had nothing to eat for hours and hours. Too scared to sleep, I used every thread of strength to stay on the vibrating shelf. The alternative was to fall onto the speeding tarmac, or to be mangled by the engine. The fumes and noise gave me a terrible headache. My skull felt like an eggshell. I was cold and starving.

The hissing wheels sent filthy spray splattering in and soon I was wet through and spiky-looking. Ellen would not want me, I thought in despair. I was hardly cuddly and appealing.

It was dark when I felt the lorry slowing down. Exhausted, I now lay stretched out limply, at the mercy of every bump in the road, and when at last the lorry stopped, I just lay there, drinking in the silence and stillness. I hurt all over.

I dragged myself out. My legs were wobbly, and it was still raining. The lorry had parked outside a supermarket, but there were houses nearby. I sniffed the air. I could smell the delicious scent of a cake baking. Using my senses, I knew this was coming from Ellen's kitchen.

Trotting from one garden to the next, I made my way along the road until I came to an iron gate set deep in a thick hedge. I could smell the sparrows who were snuggled up in there, lucky things. They were asleep while I was wide awake, covered in oil, shivering and homeless. Now the rain was pelting down, covering the road in puddles. My little paws were drenched and freezing cold. Flashes of lightning and echoing booms of thunder frightened me as I cowered under the hedge. There was no way through, so I squeezed under the gate. Despite the rain I knew I must go out into the middle of the lawn to attract Ellen's attention, and came face to face with the four staring windows and big brown door of a house.

'You have to meow as loud as you can. Now,' said my angel.

So I did. Feeling small and dirty and spiky, I let rip with the meows. I wouldn't have believed an exhausted kitten could make such a noise. My voice echoed all over the housing estate, and soon a window opened above me, and a face looked down. It was her. My beloved Ellen.

'What on earth is going on?' Ellen leaned out and saw me. Terribly ashamed of my appearance, I stuck my tail up, which is a cat's way of smiling.

'Oh look, there's a tiny kitten! I'm going down.'

Ellen picked me up and cuddled me against her heart, I could feel its soothing rhythm through my fur, and she could evidently feel mine for she said, 'Your little heart is racing! Where have you come from?'

I turned my pea-green eyes to gaze into hers. They were smoky blue in the summer darkness. Ellen still had long hair the colour of barley, just like I remembered. I patted it with my paw, intrigued to find it had become crinkly and fuzzed out around her head. Love glowed in her eyes, but her cheeks were thinner, and her hands felt different as she stroked me. They were tense and quick, less inclined to linger, and the healing light which used to shine around them was clouded. She seemed stressed, as if she had no time to use her healing gift. I knew that a storm was gathering, a storm right inside of Ellen. She was in trouble. And I was there to help.

From now on, it was my job to protect Ellen and to

stay by her side through thick and thin. This was my first chance to try and ease her pain and so, with exquisite slowness, I turned my head sideways to touch noses.

'Oh you little darling!'

That was the moment of bonding. As the clock struck midnight the rain began to fall in long needles of silver. Many times after that night I heard Ellen tell people how she had found me on midsummer night in a thunderstorm.

'What a scruffy little object!'

A man stood there, emanating resentment, and outside that was a hard cocoon of humour. He didn't fool me.

'You must bond with Joe too,' said the angel.

I hesitated, feeling afraid of the huge pink nose on Joe's face. What if it sneezed? But I managed another nose touch and eye gaze. He did like cats, and he was stroking me gently. But I was not comfortable with those gingery eyes. They were too bright. Bright but not smiling.

'He's covered in black stuff!'

Ellen put me down quickly and there were smears of oil from the lorry over her pale blue T-shirt. I paraded into the kitchen leaving little dark paw marks, my tail up straight with a kink at the top.

'What a skinny little tail,' said Joe.

'He's in such a mess, poor little thing.' Ellen was

nearly crying as she realised the state I was in. 'Let him eat something first. Then I'll give him a warm bath and dry him off.'

Joe groaned.

'Here we go again,' he said. 'I suppose you'll be up half the night pampering him. I'm going to grab another beer and head back to bed.'

He opened the fridge and took out a black and gold can. I meowed, thinking it was going to be milk for me. Then he said something alarming.

'Don't let Jessica see him. She'll have him for breakfast.'

Who, I wondered, was Jessica? A dog? A cross neighbour? Another cat?

A cold feeling of betrayal washed over me. In the kitchen was a dish with 'PUSSY' on it and some half-eaten food. I collapsed on the floor, my heart pitter-pattering against the blue and white tiles. My bones ached and my wet fur felt heavy. The burning taste of oil was on my tongue. I felt like giving up.

After coming all that way, Ellen already had a cat.

Another cat had got there first!

CHAPTER
TWO

ANOTHER CAT GOT THERE FIRST

After a horrible bath, a long drink of milk and a good night's sleep, I was feeling more positive. Especially when I awoke to find myself lying on the amber velvet cushion.

'Cats always love this cushion,' Ellen had said, putting me on it so gently after she had dried me with a fluffy towel. 'It belonged to my mum. You go to sleep little cat, and in the morning we'll find out who you belong to.'

But first, there was Jessica.

Jessica was the naughtiest cat I'd ever met. She was black and white, silky and cute with pink pads which she enjoyed flaunting, making out she was washing them. But when I saw her challenging buttercup eyes, I fell in love with her instantly. I felt intimidated by her, and a bit jealous; I could sense that she was tough and powerful, but she was gorgeous too, and I wanted her to be my friend. I could see that behind Jessica's confident exterior was a charming little cat who wanted to be loved. Already my mind was planning how to befriend her. I wanted to curl up with her in her basket, and feel her sleek warm body against mine. But I was still a kitten, and right now I longed to be allowed to play with her. Being bossed around by Jessica would be hard, but give me six months and I'd be the boss, and, hopefully, her lover.

'You wretched cat. GET OUT!'

What a shock. Could that really be Ellen's sweet soft voice shrieking like that? At me? Kittens can move even faster than cats, and I shot straight under the piano, despite being mid-yawn.

I stayed under the piano and watched the commotion as Ellen evicted Jessica and cleaned up the mess she had made in bringing a dead bird through the cat flap. This was the first of many such episodes. Jessica was outrageous. She tore up carpets, shredded furniture, and bolted her food, especially if she'd stolen it. And if she was shut outside she would rap imperiously on the window, and glare with square eyes until she was let in. Worst of all, she scratched Ellen's young son John and made him cry, and the crying started Ellen worrying. Then Ellen's worrying sent Joe into a temper.

On that first morning I felt clean and optimistic. This was my old home where I'd shared Ellen's childhood. My desire to see the stairs was overwhelming and I longed for Ellen to open the door into the hall. Persuading humans to open doors is achieved by sitting elegantly close to the door with your chin tilted up. Keep gazing at the handle and eventually they will get the message. It's telepathy at its most basic.

'He wants to explore.'

Joe opened the door for me. He obviously liked cats.

Walking into the hall was breathtaking. I remembered the fun we'd had in this lovely house. Those incredible stairs were still there, and they were perfect. To a kitten born in a bungalow, stairs were the ultimate in dry cat gymnasiums and power perches. The best spot was the post halfway up where the stairs turned left. From here you could see out of the landing window, sunbathe, and get attention from whoever came up or down. The scent told me that Jessica had already claimed it, and I soon discovered how cheekily she sat there, reaching out a draconian paw to swipe anyone who failed to acknowledge her as they passed by.

Jessica didn't want to share the stairs with me at first, but she couldn't resist showing off, streaking upstairs like a rocket. There she liked to lie in wait for me with her chin on the carpet and do a star-shaped pounce at me which was scary. The adrenalin was addictive. As I settled into my new home, Jessica and I would spend wild evenings pelting up and down stairs with flat ears and loopy tails, our flying paws thundering on the carpet. 'Mummy, LOOK!' John squealed when we started chasing each other up and down, making all three of them laugh at us, until the house was full of flying cats and giggling.

The happiness filled the walls with diamond stars and, when we finally slept, the house hummed contentedly. 'It's just the fridge humming,' Jessica said, but I knew it wasn't. Jessica was a switched-off adult cat. She had disapproving whiskers. I was young and still attuned to the spirit world. Happiness was definitely a cloud of singing stars, an energy you could generate.

As much as I loved my new home, naturally I was jealous of Jessica. Day and night my brain echoed with the thought, I am Ellen's cat. Not you. It's all wrong. Being an advanced cat, I tried to stay cool, but it hurt.

Seeing Jessica on Ellen's lap was almost more than I could bear. One day, whilst Jessica was curled up on her knee, I sat on the floor and stared at Ellen, feeling jealous and lonely. Her eyes shone back at me thoughtfully, and she reached down and lifted me up onto her shoulder.

'Are you a jealous little cat?' she crooned. 'There's no need to be, darling. I love you to bits and I hope you can stay with us.'

I heard Jessica growl, but Ellen just stroked her until she was quiet again.

'You're very beautiful,' whispered Ellen, looking at me. 'And you're like the cat I had when I was a child. Don't you worry, you little sweetheart, I'm going to look after you, and there's enough love for both you and Jessica.'

After that, I felt much better. I purred and buried my face in the soft glittery scarf Ellen was wearing.

My best move was making friends with John. He hated Jessica and screamed if she went near him, and he even ran away from strange cats in the street, running as fast as his little legs would carry him. Jessica had made him frightened of all cats.

So I spent a long time purring and rubbing against John as he sat playing on the floor. I never messed with his Lego or ran off with his teddy bear like Jessica did. I didn't want to make John cry, so I approached him gently, always purring, and one day he stretched out his little hand and touched my fur. I crept close and pretended to go to sleep curled up against his legs, still purring of course. John kept very still and began to stroke me.

'Nice cat,' he said to Ellen.

'He's not like Jessica. He's a kind, loving cat,' Ellen said, and after that John wanted to hold me and even play with me. I'd made a big effort to be good, and it was worth it.

'We're going to keep you, little cat,' Ellen told me joyfully a week later. 'No one has claimed you. We'd better give you a name.'

I looked squarely into her eyes and radiated 'Solomon' to her. To my surprise she got it right. Ellen really was quite psychic.

'I'll call you Solomon,' she said, 'because you're so wise. You are exactly like the cat I had as a child, and he was called Solomon. You don't make trouble like Jessica. I'm so glad we can keep you.'

In that golden moment I understood the wisdom of the angel. She had planned for me to take that long journey and arrive on Ellen's lawn looking pathetic. Even if I'd been born in the same street, Ellen would not have come looking for me since she already had Jessica. Appealing to Ellen's motherly need to shelter a lost kitten had ensured me a place in her home and in her heart.

I couldn't believe that this slim, stressed woman with dark circles under her eyes had once been a free spirit, a happy child who would dance barefoot on the lawn or who loved putting on her beloved pink ballet shoes and twirling all over the house, over the beautifully polished wood floors which were now covered in a tatty old carpet. I'd encouraged her by scampering about, making her laugh while she was dancing, and watching her eyes sparkle with creative energy.

I wondered why Ellen never danced now. She didn't play the piano either. One day when Joe was out and John was asleep, I sat on it and just looked at Ellen. I knew she was telepathic so I sent her my thoughts. It worked.

'Are you trying to tell me something, Solomon?' she asked.

I put my chin on the polished top of the piano and I could sense the silent strings inside, waiting to be played. I dreamed of the rippling music Ellen used to play when she was a child, and sent the dream into her mind.

She looked at the clock, then sat down and opened the lid. I was thrilled. My fur tingled as I waited for the music to begin.

It didn't work out as I'd expected.

Ellen sat there with her long fingers over the black and white keys, frozen and silent. Then, she slammed the lid down and burst into tears. She flung herself onto the sofa, sobbing and sobbing.

Horrified, I crept close to her, purring and licking the tears from her hot cheeks. It was all I could do.

I wanted to understand, so I remembered my previous life and why Ellen had cried when she was a child. When Ellen was ten years old, I'd wanted to give her a present to show how much I loved her. I knew she liked robins because there were cards all over her bedroom with pictures of them. So early one morning I headed out into the frosty garden and caught one for her. As I ran up the stairs with the robin's soft body in my mouth, I was excited. It was the first bird I'd ever caught, and I was going to put it right on Ellen's bed for her. A real robin!

Ellen was sitting up in bed, waiting for me as usual. I put the robin down with the greatest care on the duvet in front of her and sat back, satisfied with my act of giving.

But instead of saying thank you, Ellen burst into tears. Her mum came running in and gasped when she saw the robin lying on her little girl's pink duvet.

Ellen cradled it in her small hands, sobbing and sobbing. 'Look at his lovely colours,' she cried, stroking the robin's breast with one finger. 'His breast is orange, not red. Look at his tiny feet all curled up. And he feels so warm. Look at his beak, and his sweet little face. Oh Mummy, he'll never sing again will he? He's dead.' Ellen howled in grief. 'I can't make him fly again.'

She looked up and saw me sitting there. 'You horrible cat, I HATE you. Go away!'

Her mum picked me up. 'That's not fair, Ellen. It's natural for cats to catch birds, isn't it, Solomon? He thought he was bringing you a present.'

She tried to take the robin away, but Ellen sobbed even harder. 'No Mummy. I've got to look after him, even if he's dead.'

Later, I watched in astonishment as she wrapped the dead robin in layers of rainbow tissue paper and put him in a cardboard box. When her mum wasn't looking she took the bread knife from the kitchen, dug a hole in the ground under a rose bush, and buried the gift-wrapped robin. Ellen didn't stop crying all day, but she did forgive me when I cuddled up to her, purring. It taught me a lesson I would remember forever.

But I didn't understand why she was crying now, over the piano! I soon found out though when Ellen began to talk to me quietly, her speech interrupted by sobs.

'I love music so much, Solomon. But I can't do it now. I'm too exhausted. Music feeds my soul you see, and I can't do it in fragments of time. It has to be *total*, so that I disappear into it. And I've got painful memories of it too. Mum was always pushing me to perform for people, and she'd get so angry because I just couldn't. I used to freeze. Then she would punish me by locking the piano, or taking my ballet shoes away.'

We both looked up at the pair of faded pink ballet shoes hanging under the mirror on the wall.

'It was the same with ballet. She and my teacher wanted me to perform. And it wasn't about *performing*, Solomon,' she said passionately, stroking my fur very fast. 'It– it was about *joy*. Like you and Jessica when you play on the stairs. It's pure joy and fun.'

I sat up and looked at her for a long time, trying to show her that I understood. I kissed her on the nose and purred into her soft ear. That made her smile, and she said, 'Were you that cat, Solomon? Were you?' I did a loud purr-meow. 'I do believe you are the same cat, come back to me. We'll be friends forever, Solomon, won't we?'

She got up and walked over to the piano.

'Maybe I will play a bit – for John,' she said, and stroked the lid thoughtfully. 'And for you. But there's not time right now.'

I knew Ellen was unhappy. Often she'd sit in the garden so tired that she would almost fall off her chair. She coped patiently with John's lively, bubbling personality. She was always there for him, playing with him, reading him stories and laughing with him. Ellen's mother love was too strong for her own good. If John hurt himself she panicked, and if he was ill she always thought he was going to die. She worried about him so much.

'Why isn't she happy?' I asked my angel one morning. I'd climbed onto a post in the garden to catch the morning sunshine on my fur.

'She's frightened.'

'Of Joe?'

'Yes – but she is also frightened of being homeless and starving. Because she is a mum, she's very vulnerable, she has to protect and feed her child and provide a home for him. The man is not wise. He's getting into debt.'

When the angel explained to me what debts were,

the anxiety started. I could lose *my* home. I was still only a kitten. Who would feed me? Would I be able to stay here and become Jessica's lover?

Then the angel used the word 'repossession', and explained what that meant. Bailiffs could take Ellen's lovely home away, and evict the family into the street.

I climbed down from the post feeling old and responsible, a big burden for a kitten. I didn't want to talk to the angel any longer. Being spiritual seemed increasingly irrelevant in this earth life. Survival was paramount. It went something like this: get Kitekat. Keep warm and dry. Keep fur clean. Don't go on other cats' territories. Be assertive with dogs. Stay out of Jessica's basket. Get humans to open doors for us. Resist climbing the curtains. Forgive humans when they step on you. Resist thieving cheese off the table even if Jessica does it. And so on. It didn't seem to leave much time for loving Ellen.

But love was all I had to offer.

So I swanned into the kitchen with my fur radiating love, and enjoyed eye contact with Ellen. She scooped me up at once, hugging me against her heart. Alarmed to hear the heartbeat unusually loud and fast, I leaned my cheek against her chest and purred endlessly. As I turned my head, I saw Joe standing on the other side of the room, arms folded, his eyes glittering with menace.

'Anyway Solomon LOVES me,' Ellen said defiantly to Joe. His aura was dense with anger and prickly like a teasel. I could feel its destructive power in Ellen's pretty kitchen. John was sitting on his plastic tractor in the doorway, looking anxiously at his parents.

I tried to stay calm while Ellen clutched me too tightly as Joe shouted at her. He sounded like a dog barking in a concrete kennel. The pain in my ears was terrible, but I concentrated on purring, knowing I was protected by angelic light. The shouting filled the kitchen and spread through the house like smoke, going under doors, into corners and up the stairs. It permeated everything; the apples in the fruit bowl, the cosy cushions, the clocks, the bright sunny bedrooms. Then it exploded into the street in a shower of glass.

'No Joe. Stop it. JOE!' Ellen screamed, and put me down. I ran under a chair, terrified by the crack and crunch of Joe kicking the front door with his boot. His ginger hair and red face made him look like a man on fire, and his eyes were bleak slits of pain. Saliva gathered at the corners of his mouth.

'Shut up! Shut up screaming you silly cow or I'll give you something to really scream about.' Joe turned on Ellen, muscles quivering, breathing fast, his skin sweating.

'We can't afford a new door, Joe. Don't do this, PLEASE!'

'And why can't we afford a new door?' Joe raged. 'Because *you* insisted on giving up your job, didn't you?

Selfish cow!'

'I wanted to look after John whilst he's little,' said Ellen, glaring right back at Joe. 'You promised me you were going to get a job, didn't you?'

Joe hunched his shoulders and clenched his teeth. He towered over Ellen, shuffling closer and closer.

'Shut *up*,' he hissed, 'or I'll smash that smug face of yours and then I'll get some peace from your endless nagging, woman.'

Ellen went quiet. She went limp against the wall, and slid to the floor, her hands over her ears. Joe stamped his foot, and grinned when she jumped. It startled me too, so much that I wailed in fright. I thought Joe was going to kill my lovely Ellen.

I had to do something.

So I walked out from under the chair and sat between them, facing Joe. I yowled and looked right into Joe's eyes, a hard cat stare, a power stare that I didn't know I had until that moment. I could feel my angel filling my aura with a burning light.

'Don't get nasty,' she said. 'Just sit there.'

Joe turned and left, slamming the door so hard that the whole house vibrated and the remaining shards of glass crashed into the hall.

'I'll kill the pair of you,' he bellowed as he headed out.

Ellen picked me up and wept into my fur.

'What are we going to do, Solomon? What are we going to DO?'

I just kept my head down and carried on purring into Ellen's heart. She seemed frozen. Nothing I did made any difference. Perhaps that first row was the most difficult, at least it was for me anyway. And through it all Jessica was out in the garden, shamelessly chasing butterflies. For once I envied her ability to detach herself from family upsets. I made a mental note that detachment was a skill to be acquired in another lifetime. Right now I felt hopelessly inadequate, especially when Ellen put me down and picked up John, who was crying.

'What did Daddy do?' he was wailing.

'He kicked the door in.'

'It's broken!' John wailed even louder. 'And the foxes will get in.'

'We can mend it darling. Calm down. Daddy's gone out now.'

'Has Daddy gone away forever?'

'No.'

'He said he was.'

'He won't. He'll be back. You'll see,' soothed Ellen, but her eyes were sad and frightened.

'Jessica's got a butterfly!' shrieked John. He wriggled out of Ellen's arms and both of them rushed into the garden. I didn't understand why Ellen felt she had to rescue a butterfly when her own wings were broken.

Exhausted by the rowing, I crawled onto my favourite cushion to doze through the morning. Blessed sleep took me quickly into the spirit world.

'How are you doing, Solomon?'

The sight of my angel's beaming face stopped me moaning too much. The feelings of inadequacy and the pain in my ears melted into a stream of bright stars that healed my confusion. It was hard, my angel agreed, but warned me it would get worse, and in between the bad times I must concentrate on eating, playing and building myself into a strong cat.

Refreshed and brave again, I awoke at noon to the silence of an empty house. I yawned and stretched, and walked into every room with my tail up, expecting to find Ellen. Even Jessica was nowhere to be seen. A plate of cat food was in its usual place in the kitchen so I ate most of it, thinking it had an odd metallic flavour. Rabbit, it said on the tin. Tin-flavoured rabbit. Well, it was different.

I considered braving the cat flap, but it was too heavy for a kitten like me, only three months old, and it had a way of snapping shut on my tail. I decided to go upstairs to look for Ellen.

The hall was full of broken glass, and the door had been mended with a piece of cardboard and parcel tape. John's room was empty, and so was the bathroom, but Ellen's bedroom door was shut. I sat outside it staring, trying to use my psi sense to find out if she was inside, but apparently she wasn't. A few meows brought no result so I ran downstairs and jumped onto the lounge windowsill, and there, to my amazement, was Ellen. My fur stood on end, my tail bushed out like a bottlebrush. What I saw was so strange.

Ellen was inside a silver door, about the size of the puss flap. She had shrunk to the size of a blackbird. I stared and stared, not daring to move in case it happened to me. It was definitely Ellen. She had blonde hair and she was smiling, her eyes were full of light. Then I noticed something that made my fur even stiffer. *Only* her head was there in that silver door, the rest of her was missing. Spooked, I looked carefully behind the silver door and *nothing was there*. I tried to touch noses with her but a glassy screen was across the door. I sat down, feeling I mustn't take my eyes off her, and waited for her to come out.

I heard the puss flap slam and Jessica came in with a dead starling in her mouth. She dumped half of it in the kitchen and half of it under the sofa before seeing me up there staring at Ellen in the silver door.

'What are you all blown up about?' she asked. 'You look like a hedgehog.'

'Something terrible has happened to Ellen.'

Very few cats ever master the art of laughing. I certainly couldn't. But Jessica knew exactly how to curl up her mouth, spark her eyes and roll on the floor as if she were laughing.

'That's a *picture*,' she explained. 'It's not really Ellen. It's a flat image on a piece of something.'

'I don't understand.'

'Humans have *lots* of them.' Jessica sounded bored and scathing. 'Haven't you ever noticed them? Look at that flat barn owl on the wall. And there are flat rabbits on the wall in John's room. And there's a flat horse at the top of the stairs. I don't bother looking at them any more.'

I did look at the flat barn owl and felt quite spooked by it, and angry with Jessica for laughing at me. I pounced on her from the windowsill and we wrestled, squealing on the floor. Then she chased me up the curtains. At that moment, in walked Ellen – the *real* Ellen, not the flat version. I was pleased to see her but she was not pleased to see me at the top of the curtains. That was our ill-timed mistake. The skin around her eyes looked red and her aura was dark. I wanted to love her but she shooed me into the garden along with Jessica, and a few minutes later half of the dead starling came sailing out too.

I hated Jessica for getting me into trouble. Hate was something I should not be feeling. It was *bad*. It upset my stomach and clouded my vision so that I couldn't tune in to my angel. Mist surrounded me. Earth mist. Hate mist. How to get out of it, I didn't know.

In this environment I could soon have lost touch with my mission and become a boring old cat who just ate, slept and survived. I walked into the road and considered leaving. The problem with leaving is that you are likely to regret it and go back, which is even more difficult. And embarrassing, I thought, when the car returned and Joe got out, shamefaced, and padded slowly up the path, a bunch of roses in his hand.

CHAPTER
THREE

THE BAILIFF

Jessica hated the postman. She acted like a guard dog, lying in wait for him under the bushes by the front door, and pouncing on his shoelaces whenever he came near. On wet days she sat on the stairs glaring at the letter-box, and as soon as the postman pushed letters through onto the mat, she shredded them with ferocious claws. If Ellen didn't get to them first, Jessica would then use the pile of torn paper as a litter tray. Her rage was infectious. Ellen and Joe, and even little John, screamed at her, and Jessica would disappear under the sofa at speed.

She'd got a private collection of toys under there, a dead mouse, a blue and yellow Lego man, a shoelace and a Dairylea cheese portion pilfered from the kitchen table.

One morning Jessica furiously attacked a crackly brown envelope that Joe obviously wanted.

'You DEMON cat!' he roared, purple in the face as he dangled the shredded letter in his hand. As usual, he turned on Ellen. 'You would have to choose a manic moggy like her wouldn't you? Well I tell you now, that cat is going down the RSPCA.'

'No Joe,' pleaded Ellen. 'We promised to look after her, and anyway she can be a sweet little cat sometimes.'

'Sweet little cat! She's rubbish. And we can't afford to feed one cat, leave alone two.'

They were chilling words. I gazed at Joe from where I was sitting quietly on the windowsill enjoying the morning sun. Keeping calm wasn't easy, but I was managing, even when I heard the dreaded RSPCA word. Later I padded across to the sofa and coaxed Jessica out. Her eyes were huge and black, but she emerged and sat beside me in our favourite chair.

'I love you,' I said. 'And Ellen does too. But why must you tear up letters like that?'

Jessica said something surprising.

'I only tear up the brown ones. They're bills, and they make Joe bad tempered. Actually he tears them up himself, I've seen him doing it. And he hides them from Ellen.'

Jessica fascinated me. One morning I sat and watched her in the garden. She spent half her time airborne, doing reckless leaps from the garage roof to the cherry tree, then clambering up through the branches. Next she sat on the high wall and batted at swallows. The tiny birds dive bombed her, almost clipping her with a blade-like wing as they twisted out of her reach.

'Do you wish you were a bird?' I asked her.

'No.' She waited until I'd climbed through a prickly

bush to the top of the wall to be with her. 'Tiresome teenage kitten,' she growled, lashing her tail at me. She took off down to the lawn, leaving me marooned up there, meowing. She slipped through the cat flap and I figured she would be in the kitchen eating from *my* dish. Moments later she emerged with a big brick of cheese in her mouth.

'YOU PIGGING CAT!' Joe burst into the garden and saw Jessica's tail disappearing under the shed. 'Why do I bother giving you a home? I worked my hands to the bone to pay for that cheese and you go and nick it. Thieving moggy. You're nothing but trouble.'

He seized a broom and banged on the shed with it. But Jessica didn't come out. I saw Sue-next-door peering through her curtains, and I wondered where Ellen was. I felt scared on top of the wall, with Joe's voice booming all over the garden. I wanted Ellen to come and coax me down.

Horrified, I watched Joe lie down and ram the broom handle under the shed. Jessica would be killed. The shed was creaking and rocking as Joe attacked it. I looked up at Sue-next-door, who was standing firmly at the window with her arms folded, and I sent her a silent meow. She responded by rolling her eyes.

Jessica popped out from the other side of the shed, still with the cheese in her mouth, and streaked across the lawn. I saw a flash of white paws and pink pads as she cleared the fence into Sue-next-door's garden. Joe hurled the broom after her with such force that it snapped a row of tomato plants which Ellen had been growing against the sunny fence. A hot, dusty smell rose from them and green tomatoes rolled over the grass.

Joe stood there, his aura steaming. His face was red and his hands trembled. Slowly he walked over and picked up a green tomato, and looked at it in silence. He picked up the two halves of the broom, tried unsuccessfully to fit them back together, and stalked back towards the house. He walked right past me but didn't look up, and I saw big fat tears on his furious cheeks. I sensed his pain.

I wished Ellen would come back. But she didn't. Instead, a purple silence filled the garden.

Jessica had called me a 'tiresome teenage kitten' but that wasn't true. I was a healing cat. If I saw tears on human cheeks I had to do something. So I climbed down through the prickly bush, and trotted into the house with my tail up. I could tell where Joe was by the sour smell of beer. He was slumped in a corner by a pile of magazines, wiping his tears with the back of his hand, sniffing and slurping from a can. I ran to him as if he was my best friend. Being careful not to scratch him, I walked nicely along his leg and up his torso to his heart. It was bang-banging in there, and his arms were shaking. He looked at me in surprise.

As soon as we had eye contact, I gazed into his soul and purred. I licked the salty tears from his face, but more of them came zigzagging down.

'Oh Solomon,' he whispered. 'How can you love a bad-tempered bastard like me?'

I purred louder, stretching my paws over his heart, and rubbed my head against his bristly chin.

'The truth is, Solomon,' he said, 'I don't like myself one bit. Everything I do goes wrong. I'm no good. In fact, I'm bloody doomed.'

I pretended to go to sleep and let him talk, his hot hand smoothing my fur, and after a while he quietened down and my angel came close, shining her light over us as we dozed in the chair.

'You're doing a great job, Solomon,' she said.

After Joe's outburst I needed another cat to curl up with. Jessica didn't come back until it was dark and everyone had gone to bed, even the swallows. Moonlight spilled in through the window and polished her sleek fur as she came in. I ran to meet her. She condescended to touch noses with me, and I got to look into her eyes. In the night they were deep saucers of green, and her whiskers glistened magnificently each side of her little pink nose. To me she was exquisitely beautiful. Why didn't she want to be friends with me?

I followed her to her basket, but she wouldn't let me in there. Sensing she was tired, I sat watching her. All I wanted was to curl up against her silky warmth.

'Go away,' she hissed. 'You smell like that sour stuff Joe drinks.'

'I've been lying on him,' I said. 'Healing him.'

Jessica looked at me out of slitty eyes.

'Traitor,' she said. 'You should have been scratching him after the way he treated me.'

'I don't scratch humans. I'm a healing cat.'

'Poof!' Jessica curled up into a silken mound and closed her eyes as if I wasn't there. Confused, I watched her go to sleep, and respected her peace. I didn't dare to even put one paw inside her cosy basket; I spent the night hunched on the cold floor just to be near her.

In the morning her eyes were buttercup yellow again, and when she yawned, I saw the curl of her tongue and the pink roof of her mouth. She looked surprised and not pleased to see me there. We touched noses and it made me buzz all over with excitement. Her eyes hardened and she hissed at me, but not before I'd seen the sadness that lurked behind those golden eyes. Sadness – and anger. I wanted to know where it had come from, but Jessica wouldn't talk to me.

I'd fallen in love with a cat who didn't want me.

One evening Joe came through the back door with a bottle of wine and a pizza in a box. He had a rare smile on his face.

'Where did you get this?' Ellen asked.

'Stop frowning, Ellen,' Joe said, and he fished into his back pocket and took out some cash. 'I've got a JOB!'

'A *job*? Oh wow, that's amazing.' Ellen's face lit up with a happy smile. She gave Joe a hug and pushed his hair out of his eyes. 'Doing what?'

'Don't get too excited, it's only casual work – in the bar at the pub. Three nights a week.'

'Great,' said Ellen, 'but …'

'Don't give me that face, Joe said. 'I won't be drinking if *that's* what you're worried about. I'm going to look after *my* family.'

Ellen sighed and opened the big pizza box.

'Hmm. Yum. Do you want a little bit, Solomon?'

The times when Joe went to work were peaceful for us, golden summer evenings in the garden, with John, Jessica and me racing around while Ellen worked on a little flower bed. On wet evenings I managed to persuade her to play the piano again. John got so excited, dancing and squealing and singing little songs. Even Jessica enjoyed it and she came and lay beside me on top of the piano, feeling the ripples of music and watching Ellen's aura brightening as she played.

'Will it be all right now that Joe has a job?' I asked my angel. For a moment she was silent. Then she looked at me sadly and new colours flickered in the light that shone around her; deeper blues and purples.

'No,' she said. 'It's too little, too late.'

Summer passed and the lawn thundered with falling apples. Ellen and John walked round the hedges picking lush blackberries and putting them into bags, and I insisted on going with them, always with my tail up very straight.

'Like a snorkel,' Ellen laughed as I dashed through the long grass.

But she didn't like me following her to the shop. After my trip in the lorry, traffic really scared me, and if I tried to follow Ellen along the main road it involved panicky dives into strange hedges and gardens. I followed Ellen everywhere. I would not let her out of my sight. Sometimes she shut me in and then I sat at the window like a sentry awaiting her return.

Ellen was changing. Often she was angry and frightened, and exhausted by the frequent rows with Joe. But she always welcomed my love, and the supply of Kitekat continued. I was cuddled and brushed and sprinkled with flea powder. She even gave me vitamins and the occasional egg. I grew into a glossy tomcat.

It was a cold winter night when Jessica finally let me into her basket. I held my breath and stepped in gingerly. Hardly daring to hope that this was happening, I silently eased myself close to her. She'd had a bad day and I knew she needed me, as I needed her. For once she didn't push me away. She growled a little, and purred with me, and I sensed her silent need for a friend, a friend who loved her no matter what.

Blissfully, I lay against her warm silky coat and let the stars of happiness cluster around us. After that night we always slept together with our soft paws intertwined. Jessica liked to lie with her chin on my neck and I loved to feel her there. Together we made a kind of music, love music made of little purrs and sighs and squeaks. Sometimes I slid my paw around her glossy back, and when the morning sun shone through the window, I lay dreaming, watching the colours of the sun glint on her black fur.

Winter passed, and when spring came I was the boss cat. Jessica was now very flirty with me. She provoked me into wild chases, through the raspberry canes and up the cherry tree and over the garage roof. We mated all over the place, on the neighbour's lawn, in the vegetable garden, even in the middle of the road. But the best time was on top of the tumble drier in the utility room, when it was running. Ellen opened the door and saw us. We froze, squared our eyes, and continued. Ellen got the message, smiled and left us alone.

A month or so later Jessica became fat and heavy with my kittens.

Soon she was too fat to crawl under the sofa. Being pregnant calmed her down. It calmed everyone down,

including me. Jessica was contented. She left the postman alone, set up a new refuge for herself under Ellen's
bed, and on a hot night in June, Jessica gave birth all by
herself to three silky kittens. My children.

Ellen immediately moved them all downstairs to a
basket in the kitchen, but Jessica insisted on moving
them back, carrying each kitten in her mouth carefully
up the stairs. She always left the little tabby one until
last. It was a girl kitten, fluffy and very beautiful with
tinges of silver and gold in her fur.

'This is a special kitten,' said my angel, 'she's come
here to heal, like you, Solomon.' So, in those moments
before Jessica came back for her, I gave the tabby kitten
lots of love and purring. One day she opened her baby
blue eyes and looked at me as if she wanted to fix me in
her memory forever.

It was the last happy day I remember. The house felt
sunlit and peaceful. Ellen and Joe were friends, and John
was playing happily in the garden.

And that was the day the bailiff came.

I was feeling fragile because a few days ago Joe had
taken me to the vet who had put me to sleep and done
something to me to stop me making any more kittens. It
was painful, and humiliating, and I felt depressed afterwards, despite understanding the reason. I'd agreed this
in the spirit world. Being a full tomcat would distract
me from my true path. I had agreed to love Ellen and

help her through a difficult time, but if I'd known *how* difficult it would be then I might not have volunteered. Ellen had let me have my fling with Jessica first. She'd wanted Jessica to experience the joys of motherhood and for John to see the kittens born and growing up.

That was Ellen's idealistic dream.

On that warm June day my angel had alerted me at dawn. She'd shown me a picture of a man in a grey suit inside a large building with 'County Court' carved in stone letters over the door. The man had been writing Ellen's name and address on a form. My angel told me that today he was coming to our house. Ellen didn't know. I had to be there. To stay calm and keep purring. 'Remember you are a healing cat,' she said.

Joe had gone out and I had to sit up all day watching, even though I wanted to lie down after what the vet had done. By lunchtime I was worn out. No one had come. Ellen was pottering about the garden while John was splashing and squealing in a big water tub on the lawn. Eventually I fell asleep, curled up on the sunny doorstep. In my dreams bees were humming over the flowers, swallows twittered overhead and the long grass at the edge of the lawn was full of chirping grasshoppers. As I dreamed about the spirit world another sound dragged me back, heavy footsteps coming nearer. I opened one eye and saw a pair of gleaming shoes on the doorstep.

'Hello puss!' A man's hand reached down to stroke me. The bailiff!

Compared to a tiger a cat is very small. So it's no good acting like a tiger and attacking people. Cats have to be subtle and artful.

I displayed my hostility to the bailiff, completely ignoring him by staring into the distance with no response to his attempt to stroke me. After what the angel had said, it was surprising to find the bailiff was an ordinary human. But he was acting sinister.

His neck was locked stiff, his eyes icy cold and his heart encased in metal. I could hear it ticking as he knocked at the door.

Ellen opened it, carrying John who was wrapped in a blue bath towel. Her innocent eyes looked enquiringly at the bailiff.

'Double glazing?' she smiled. 'No thanks.'

'Mrs King?'

'Yes. That's me. And this is John.'

John didn't look happy, even though Ellen was bouncing him about to try and make him laugh. His solemn eyes caught mine. He knew. The bailiff's frozen aura was obvious and menacing to him.

'Mrs Ellen King?'

'Yes.' The smile was shrinking on Ellen's face.

'And your husband is Mr Joseph King?'

'Yes?'

The bailiff showed Ellen a card.

'I'm a bailiff from the county court. I have a warrant to enter your property and seize goods to the value of seventeen thousand pounds, a debt your husband owes to the bank.'

I watched Ellen's aura splintering. It was alarming. John chose that moment to start crying, and this upset Ellen. She screamed at the bailiff and her eyes were two cracks of blue fire.

'How dare you come here, threatening us? Can't you see I'm a mother with a small child? It's not *my* debt, it's HIS! I know nothing about it!'

I wormed my way into the hall and sat at Ellen's feet, puffing myself up protectively. How I wished I was a dog, an Alsatian or a Rottweiler. It's terrible having to hiss when you want to bark.

The man kept coldly repeating the same words, his voice a monotonous chant against Ellen's hysteria and John's crying. However, as Ellen's distress grew, it was John who calmed her down by putting his fat little arms around her neck.

'Mummy, talk nicely.'

Ellen's legs were shivering. The bailiff's gleaming shoes were squeaking across the doormat. My angel stood in the hall with a golden sword in her hand but no one except me could see her. Jessica was bolting upstairs with yet another kitten swinging from her mouth.

'Ellen doesn't have to let him in, Solomon,' said the angel, and for a moment I feasted on the glorious sapphire light from the angel's eyes, and basked in the energy streaming from the golden sword. I felt happy to see the angel here in our house, protecting Ellen. Happy, and then sad again, devastated that Ellen couldn't see the angel and wasn't comforted by any small gesture from me. The limitation of being a mortal cat was more painful than I could bear. In the pain of my helplessness I did a dreadful thing. In front of the angel, I ran away.

In bitter shame I climbed as high as possible, up the garden wall, across the garage and onto the roof. With my tail dragging, I crept up the tiles and sat against the chimney staring far away across the fields to the dark blue hills. I wanted to go home to the spirit world. Seeing the angel had unsettled me, and made me homesick.

The sun warmed the brick chimney, and scorched my glistening black fur. My whiskers felt hypersensitive, and the tips of my ears burned. I, Solomon, was a failure. Being a cat was too difficult. Sometimes my sleek black body was enjoyable, when it belted up and down stairs or flopped blissfully into a chair, especially when Ellen was stroking me. But inside I was a big shining lion of a soul, too big to fit inside a small black cat.

When I heard Joe's car squealing to a halt outside the house, I sat up anxiously. He got out with a slam that sent flakes of rust flying from his car. His brows glowered at the bailiff's shiny van in passing, and his aura was purple.

After he'd gone inside, an ominous silence followed, with not even a murmur of voices audible.

'Look at that cat on the roof!'

'Perhaps he can't get down.'

The children were coming home from school, a group of them who often stroked me. Just now I really needed their love and it was tempting to go down. But the front door was opening and Joe appeared, looking like an unexploded bomb. The bailiff was with him, and Ellen was there with her shoulders hunched. She still had John's towel in her hands, twisting it into a rope.

'We'll expect your settlement in seven days,' the bailiff said, handing Joe a white paper. Joe passed it roughly to Ellen.

'YOU had better have this.'

The 'you' was filled with hateful energy. Joe was on the brink of a storm. Sure enough, as soon as the bailiff had gone, the shouting began.

'YOU get inside!'

'It's not my FAULT,' Ellen screamed as the door slammed shut.

I crept close against the chimney, moving around onto the cool shadow. Thunder always scared me. Now the thunder was inside the house. Even the roof trembled. People in the street paused to listen, turning frightened faces towards the house.

'He's at it again,' said Sue-next-door to a woman who was walking past. She rolled her eyes. 'Poor girl. I don't know how she puts up with him, and she's got that lovely baby too.'

It was worrying to think of little John in there. Maybe I should have gone into his bedroom and given him some love. And poor Jessica. How wise she had been to have her kittens under the bed. Ellen had moved them twice, and Jessica had determinedly moved them back again one by one. What guts. I imagined her cowering under the bed, suckling my children and reassuring them, during my lonely vigil on the roof. Jessica needed extra food and support at this time. Maybe I should catch a mouse and take it up to her. The sun was turning amber, it must be round about teatime.

'That cat's still up there.'

'If he's not down before dark I'm going to knock their door.'

The two women marched past with a dog trailing complacently behind. Gazing at the blue hills brought me to dreaming instead of worrying. In my meditative state I remembered the heaven world, and suddenly in my mind I was back there, sitting on iridescent cushions of grass and purring out millions of stars. Then I purred them in again. Power stars. Love that would be needed. And they were all for Ellen, every single one.

The sound of the front door opening jolted me back

to earth. Joe was leaving – again. He was hurling books and clothes into the car, and pairs of boots and a kettle. There was no sign of Ellen. Not a sound. Not a cry from John or a meow from Jessica.

The car wouldn't start.

Joe sat there fuming, turning the key repeatedly, but there was not a spark of life. I worried that Joe would go inside again and take it out on Ellen.

Eventually he started to push the car on his own. Curtains twitched at windows but no one came out to help. The car gathered speed down the sloping cul-de-sac, with Joe lumbering behind. Anger really fires humans into athletic improbability. In a jumble of legs and elbows Joe overtook the car and leaped into the driving seat. The car fired up with a bang, roared down the cul-de-sac, turned and roared back even faster, and was finally gone, almost airborne, heading for the motorway.

The first door to open was Sue-next-door. I hurried down from the roof to be with her as she tapped nervously on Ellen's door. Sue's legs had jeans and pink fluffy slippers. We both stared at the door, as if staring would make it open. The fur on my tail started to bristle because I was so anxious. It was embarrassing.

'Solomon, what a great big tail!' Sue had a kindly voice, very reassuring. She bent down to stroke me, but I couldn't concentrate on responding. The silence from the house was so spooky.

'Supposing he's killed Ellen,' I thought.

Sue was calling through the letterbox.

'Ellen! It's Sue-next-door. Are you all right?'

We waited, listening intently, and at last there was a sound from inside the house, a tinkling of glass, and Ellen came slowly to the door. She stood there trembling, looking up and down at both of us with eyes like mouse holes.

'I'm all right,' she sighed and lifted her tired face into a defiant smile. 'And I'm glad he's gone!'

'Is John all right?'

'John is fine. Believe it or not he slept through it all.'

'Has he hurt you?'

'Not physically. He threatened to kill us both. But he loves John. He wouldn't touch John. It's me. He blames me for everything.'

Ellen began to sob from deep down in her stomach. Sue guided her to an armchair while I padded around with my tail up, inappropriately. Sue was comforting Ellen so I shot upstairs to check on Jessica.

Communal purring rippled from under the bed where she lay stretched out. All three of the kittens were vigorously suckling, their little pink paws energetically dough punching. Their heads were like wet pebbles with buds for ears. The little tabby and white one finished feeding first and she lay gazing at me with those blue eyes, opening her mouth and doing a squeak of a meow at me. She wanted to communicate with me.

Humans are lucky to be able to cry. Cats can't do that. But in that moment I could have cried with overwhelming love and fatherly pride. I was a dad now, and the kittens would need me. There was so much to teach them, and I longed to ask them about the spirit world while it was fresh in their minds. My beautiful children. What an ego trip.

'Get out, Solomon.' Jessica growled at me. But she was too ecstatic to look fierce. She lay back, slitty eyed and purring, enjoying the experience of feeding my kittens. I retreated respectfully.

John's bedroom door was open. He was asleep, so completely still that he seemed to be made of marble. I sat down by the cot and purred, enjoying the white mist of light that surrounded the sleeping child. It was particularly strong at the head of the cot, and intense concentration showed me the shimmer of an angel who was there guarding John.

Once more I left my earthly cat body and saw where John was in his dreamtime. He was playing in a meadow with a blue balloon on a string, and all around him flowers of light twinkled and glittered in the grass. An old man was with him, a dear round-faced man with tender hands, and beaming eyes which sparkled as John ran to him, laughing. John looked so different from the serious and often-troubled toddler he was on earth. In his dreamtime he was carefree and radiant.

Ellen found me asleep in John's cot.

'You shouldn't be in here, Solomon,' she said, and gently lifted me out. She couldn't be cross with me when I cuddled up to her, purring, looking attentively into her eyes.

'Dear Solomon.' Ellen carried me over to the window and we stood admiring the evening garden, which was full of coral light and warbling blackbirds. Scents of newly mown hay drifted from the fields, and a midsummer moon was rising in the east.

'It's one year since you came. Happy birthday Solomon,' said Ellen, and tears ran down cheeks which were already red from crying.

I wanted to tell her how much I loved this sunny house and express gratitude for such a lovely home. The sun-warmed stones and the soft lawn, the cherry tree, the nice people who walked past and stroked me. The puss flap and the wonderful stairs, the kitchen full of aromatic steam, the quiet corners where I loved to sit. And best of all, my special chair with the amber cushion. I wanted to say how sad it was that Joe had smashed yet another door, and broken Ellen's china. But the house was still good. It was built upon an old cornfield and the spirit of the corn was still there inside its walls. The house was full of Ellen's love and John's playing, and now my wonderful kittens were purring upstairs. No matter what Joe did, the house would always be good. I'd lived two lives here now, and it was home.

These thoughts amplified my purring, during the time of sunset with Ellen. Sadly she couldn't understand them, but I could understand her human speech and what she was saying came as a deep shock to me.

'We've got to sell our house, Solomon. We're leaving,' she sobbed. 'And I don't even know if we can keep you.'

CHAPTER
FOUR

LEAVING HOME

I didn't want to share the dreaded cat basket with Jessica. Joe had caught her by the scruff, bundled her inside and slammed it shut before she could reverse out. Jessica was good at reversing. Now she was in a cage. She turned around and stared out at everyone, her beautiful eyes desperate. I sat close to the basket, kissing her through the hard iron bars, trying to calm her down, but she wouldn't be pacified. She was frightened, and broken hearted. Her three lovely kittens had gone out in that same cat basket the day before, and Joe had come back with it empty.

'You did take them to the cat sanctuary didn't you?' Ellen asked.

'Course I flaming did. What d'you take me for?' Joe said angrily. He was in an ugly mood, slumped on the sofa with his head in his hands. 'Just leave me alone, will you? It's bad enough losing our home without you starting.'

I looked at him sceptically. I felt he was lying. What had he done with our kittens? I couldn't help feeling

63

that the little tabby and white one, my favourite, was lost somewhere and crying for me.

We didn't know what was going on. All day we'd sat on the garden wall and watched two men carrying furniture out of the house.

Ellen wanted me in her arms when the two men were struggling with the heavy old piano. She touched it just once before they loaded it onto the lorry.

'Mum bought me that piano,' she told me. 'It's a real beauty. It's so sad to let it go like this. It's breaking my heart.'

I pushed my head into her neck, trying to tell her how well I remembered those magical hours of music when I'd sat on top of that same piano and marvelled at the stream of melodies that danced from Ellen's hands, and the rapt expression on her young face as she played. She was inside the music, living it. 'She's so gifted,' her mum would say, 'but if you ask her to play for somebody she won't! She only plays to the cat.'

Ellen's piano, the sofa, the warm hearthrug, and our favourite chair were being loaded onto a lorry, and soon our lovely house was empty. Jessica and I had crept inside and tiptoed through the bare rooms and up the stairs where we had played so joyfully. Our tails were down, our eyes big with anxiety.

Ellen ran out to the lorry and snatched the amber velvet cushion from one of the chairs.

'My mum made that,' she said fiercely to the two men. 'And you are not having it. Arrest me if you like.'

She stuck her chin in the air and glared, and one of the men just shrugged.

'Let her have it. It's only a cushion,' he said, and with one flick of his arms he closed the back of the lorry and climbed into the driving seat.

Ellen stood on the lawn clutching the amber cushion, watching the lorry drive away, her cheeks streaming with tears. Joe was in the doorway, his eyes black with anger, his arms folded across his chest. He roared a swear word after the lorry.

'Don't start,' said Ellen.

'Don't *you* start.'

I could see that Joe was struggling to control his temper. The air around him was steaming with it. Right inside the cloud of anger was a burning pain. It was hurting Joe, and it would hurt Ellen. I was torn between staying with Jessica, comforting Ellen, or calming Joe, and I chose Joe. The most important thing was to stop his anger exploding. First I imagined myself surrounded by the sparkle of healing stars, then I ran to him with my tail up and purred my loudest purr.

'Oh Solomon.' He stooped and picked me up. I leaned against his chest, gazed into his eyes and something magical happened. Big fat tears began to pour down Joe's cheeks, into my fur, and the cloud of anger drifted away through the garden and over the rooftops.

I expected to be rewarded with a tin of sardines or a long cuddle, but Joe carried me to the cat basket where Jessica was shredding the rug. Somehow Joe managed to stuff me in there with her, and shut the cage door before I could turn round. Then he lifted the basket, swung it into the back of the car and shut the door.

Something terrible was happening. I realised that either we were going to the vet or the RSPCA. I sat down, pressing myself against the cage door. The healing stars had vanished and I felt trapped.

Ellen had put John into his car seat, and Sue-next-door was looking in at us.

'Goodbye Solomon and Jessica. Bye bye John,' she was saying, and then she and Ellen were hugging and crying over each other. Why was everyone crying, I wondered? It was a beautiful golden day with the first autumn leaves floating down from the cherry tree. We should be out there in the sun, playing with them.

Joe got into the driving seat and Ellen sat beside him, still clutching the amber velvet cushion.

'Here we go,' said Ellen, bravely trying to smile. 'You cats settle down. We're going on a long journey.'

As soon as the car backed out of the drive and set off down the road, Jessica started yowling. She yowled and she yowled and she wouldn't stop. Me, I would have just sat quietly since there was no escape, but I was so upset by Jessica's distress that I yowled along with her.

'They can't keep this up for two hundred miles,' said Joe. He drove grimly, and very fast. Soon we were on a motorway with heavy lorries thundering along beside me, and I was so terrified that my fur started coming out, especially where it was rubbing against the bars. It reminded me of my long trip in the oily lorry.

Humans seem to make such a mess of their lives. If I were a wild cat I would stay in one place forever and get to know it. I'd make a magnificent nest in the hedge, and make it cosy, and I'd live happily in the sunshine.

John had gone to sleep in his car seat. I could see the side of his fat little cheek and his hand flopped across his teddy bear's tummy. He looked peaceful, and so did his teddy bear, whose eyes twinkled at me as always. I figured they had got it right, accepting what was happening, so I tried to quieten down. Ellen turned around and looked into my eyes.

'It's OK, Solomon,' she said. 'I'll look after you.'

After that I did manage to doze, but Jessica's incessant yowling gave me a headache. I closed my eyes, and when I opened them everything had changed. We were on a quieter road, wandering between hills and rocks covered in heather and gorse. I could smell bracken and sheep. We'd been in the car for hours and hours, and it was raining hard. The rain swept sideways and mist rolled past the windows, thick and white, hiding everything.

'I can't see a thing,' Joe kept grumbling. Sometimes he said, 'I'll throttle that cat.'

Jessica didn't care. She had shredded the rug into a ball of string and peed on it, making her pink paws sore and red. She went on crying and crying and there was nothing I could do to comfort her.

Jessica and I were town cats. We'd both grown up on housing estates with walls and squares of garden, always with the noise of radios and children and lawn mowers. So when Joe finally stopped the car and turned off the engine, the silence, the wild smells and the furious rain of the countryside was electrifying. Quite exciting actually.

'Here we are,' said Ellen. 'This is it. Home sweet home.'

'I wish,' growled Joe.

I sat up and tried to stretch, my head bumping the top of the cage. Close to the car was a weird-looking house with a pale cream door. It was on wheels like a car.

'I don't want to live in this poxy caravan,' Joe complained, but Ellen was being cheerful, waking John up and chatting brightly.

'Come on, it's going to be lovely. We can make it nice. Now let's get these poor cats out first. We'll shut them in the end bedroom and butter their paws.'

'Butter their paws?' said John. 'Don't be silly Mummy!'

'It's what you have to do to help a cat when you move house,' explained Ellen. 'They get scared and want to run away, so you put butter on their paws and while they are licking it off they take in their new surroundings and settle down. Maybe it's an old wives' tale, but it works.'

The car door was opened, and rain came pelting in. Ellen whisked the cat basket into the caravan. It smelled of plastic, and it was freezing cold in there. She took us into a tiny bedroom, shut the door and let us out. Jessica crawled under the bed, but I was glad to cuddle up in Ellen's arms. She sat on the bed with me and we looked out of the window at the swirling mist.

'We're in Cornwall, Solomon,' she told me. 'And it's going to be lovely, you'll see. You're a Cornish cat now.'

She stroked me all over, smoothing my ruffled fur, and then she spread butter on my paws, put down a dish of water, and a plate of our favourite cat food.

'You stay here, the pair of you, and when we've unloaded the car and it's stopped raining, you can go and explore.'

Jessica stayed under the bed, but I sat up on top of a cupboard by the window and enjoyed licking the butter off my paws while I watched them unloading stuff from the car. I didn't like the feel of the caravan. It was damp, and it shook all the time, especially when Joe was walking about and John was running from room to room squealing in excitement. I didn't feel safe in there. It didn't feel like home at all. As soon as it stopped raining, I vowed to go outside and find a better place than this.

Later that evening we were allowed out of the bedroom, but the door to the outside remained firmly shut. I inspected everything, walking about nicely with my tail up. There were no stairs, and nowhere to play, no puss flap and no sofa. But I found a wide sunny windowsill and spread myself out on it. Jessica refused to take an interest in our new home. She slunk around suspiciously, her neck getting longer and longer as she peered into the tiny rooms and cupboards. Then she scrabbled at the outside door and yowled.

'Don't let her out,' Ellen called from the bedroom where she was putting John to bed. He was crying.

'I don't like it here, Mummy. I want to go back to our old home.'

'You can't, darling. It's not our house now.'

'But why, Mummy?'

Ellen kept telling him, but he wouldn't calm down and so I jumped onto his bed and lay close to him, purring.

'There – Solomon's here, and he's all right,' said Ellen.

I wasn't all right. I wanted to go back to our old house too. The wanting started as a little ache inside my heart, but I didn't let John know that. I curled up on his pillow and pretended to go to sleep until he stopped crying and snuggled down in his new bed.

'One down, two to go,' said Ellen wearily. 'Now it's Jessica's turn.'

I watched in amazement as Ellen's aura filled with stars, and the bright mist of an angel shimmered beside her. In that moment I felt proud to be her cat. Ellen had a special loving way of healing and calming any distressed creature. I remembered the times she had done it as a child, when she'd been surrounded with angels. Now I sat close, basking in the energy as if it was sunshine.

Ellen coaxed Jessica away from scrabbling at the door, picked her up and sat her on the amber velvet cushion, all the time stroking and talking in a low hypnotic voice.

'It's OK, Jessica darling. This is your home now and it's going to be fine. And your dear kittens have gone to live in kind homes. Yes I know you miss them, darling.'

Jessica was listening, her tired eyes fixed on Ellen's face, her fur gradually regaining its gloss under Ellen's gentle touch. She even started to purr, though she wasn't good at it.

'This is a tranquilliser, Jessica,' Ellen said, showing her a small white shiny tablet. 'It won't harm you, but it will help you sleep, and then you'll feel better, and in the morning you and Solomon can explore our new place.'

Ellen dipped the tablet in butter, and Jessica opened her pink mouth like a little bird. Swiftly Ellen popped the tablet onto the back of her tongue and held Jessica's mouth shut while she stroked her throat. I saw the bump of the tablet going down, and Jessica went quiet and floppy, spreading herself over the cushion.

'Phew,' said Joe. 'That was a miracle. I came close to chucking that cat out of the car today.'

'Don't send her those angry vibes, Joe,' Ellen said, her fingers still stroking the sleeping cat. 'And don't call her "that cat".'

She looked at me.

'You don't need a tranquilliser, Solomon, do you?'

I rolled onto my back, kicked my paws in the air, and looked around at her cheekily.

'No,' she said. 'Obviously not.'

The angel stayed with us all night in the creaking caravan with the rain thundering on the roof and slamming against the windows. I dozed, trying to come to terms with the big change in our lives, wondering how we could get used to this cramped caravan and the unknown world outside. I worried about Joe. What would happen if he lost his temper? In this fragile place where the cups rattled if anyone walked across the floor, there was no room for Joe's bombastic temper.

The night was dense and dark outside. No orange street lights like we'd been used to. But later in the night the rain stopped and when I pushed my head between the funny little curtains, I saw bright stars in the sky and I sat gazing at the universe and talking to my angel.

'You mustn't try to leave, Solomon, even if you don't like it. Ellen is going to need you so much. There are hard times coming, but you must stay.'

She kept repeating this, and in the morning I had made up my mind to stay and make the best of it.

But then I had a terrible shock.

I was the only one awake, sitting on the windowsill in the morning sun. I wanted to see the garden and get a sense of where we were. The caravan was up against a high hedge covered in wild plants and bramble, impossible to see what was on the other side. At the front was green space, and more caravans. Then I saw something terrifying. I sat up extra straight and my tail began to bristle like a stiff brush. The hairs stood up all along my back and up my neck, my heart raced, and I might have stopped breathing too.

Coming along the wide path towards the caravan was the most enormous fearsome-looking dog I had ever seen. It was dragging a little man who was leaning backwards, holding the lead with both hands.

The massive dog had glinty eyes and I could hear it snuffling and growling and the clickety click of its nails along the path. It trotted over to Joe's car and lifted its beefy leg to pee on the tyre. Then it looked up, saw me at the window and hurled itself at the caravan, bellowing and barking. The whole caravan shook with its power. I was petrified.

Back home we'd had a front garden with a fence and a white iron gate that kept dogs out. Here it was open space. How could I ever go outside with that dog around? I was only a young cat. I needed space to play and explore. Promising the angel that I would stay now felt like an impossible task.

My hackles gradually subsided as I crouched in the window, and this time I assessed the space in a different way. I looked for escape routes and high perches, gazing at the houses in the distance and a long road curving around the hill. I began to plan how I would escape.

CHAPTER FIVE

THAT DOG

There was no sign of the dog when Joe opened the caravan door and let us out into the sunshine. Jessica didn't hang around but streaked off across the wet grass, her tail kinked like a racehorse. She dived into the thick hedge and disappeared.

'That's the last we'll see of her,' said Joe, rather smugly.

'She'll come back,' Ellen predicted. 'She just needs to check out where she is.'

I was more cautious and Ellen picked me up and carried me, which I really appreciated. John toddled beside us, his little legs in blue plastic wellies. Leaving Joe sitting on the caravan steps swigging beer from a can, we paraded around the edge of the caravan site. From Ellen's shoulder I could see over the hedge into a copse of sycamore trees. It had secret winding paths and a mound of bare earth with gigantic holes, which looked spooky to me. What kind of creature might live in such big dark holes?

The birds were different here. There were noisy magpies and jackdaws, and the sky was full of grey and white seagulls who opened their orange beaks and dived around, screaming like police cars.

We met a woman who was hanging washing out-side her caravan. She had chunky brown elbows and a reassuring laugh, and eyes that sparkled like those of an angel. She made a fuss of John, and of me.

'Eee – isn't he bonny? I love cats.' She came right up to Ellen and put her wrinkled face close to mine. We touched noses. Sue-next-door, I thought, only she had a different name – Pam. Pam-next-door. A good person to escape to, I decided. All the way round I was check-ing out escape routes and possible hiding places; holes in the hedge, boxes under caravans and perches in trees.

'Where does the campsite owner live?' Ellen asked.

Pam pointed to a gap in the hedge where the wide path curved into the next field. 'Through there and up the slope to the far end. He's got a big house with a garden. But watch that dog. It's OK with me, but it's a bit iffy with strangers.'

'Is it loose?' asked Ellen.

'No. It's shut in the garden,' said Pam. 'But sometimes it escapes and Nick can't control it – it's bigger than he is. Oh I laugh when I see him trying to take it for a walk. Like a cart horse it is, great big feet it's got.'

I didn't understand everything Pam was saying, but I got the word dog, and began to feel uneasy. I tensed as Ellen carried me towards the house. In the wall was a black iron gate with curly patterns. I fixed my eyes on the garden beyond. I could smell it, and sense it. That dog.

'What's the matter, Solomon?' asked Ellen, holding me tighter.

'Big dog, Mummy – look,' squealed John as the dog appeared behind the gate. It didn't bark. It just loomed.

I did a dreadful thing. In my struggle to get away, I scratched Ellen's bare shoulder. Then I was flying across the grass, back the way we had come, faster than I'd ever run before, leaving the dog barking behind me. Out in a vast space with nowhere to hide, I pelted through the gap in the hedge. Which was our caravan? I didn't know. The only option was to plunge into the undergrowth.

Cornish hedges are made of stone and it was easy to crawl up inside through the brambles and nettles and then into the twiggy cover of a hawthorn tree, which was growing out of the wall. It was an awkward, prickly climb, but I went deep into its branches and sat there listening to my fast beating heart. In the distance the dog was still barking, and John was screaming. From my hiding place I watched Ellen carrying him back down the path, talking to him in her quiet way.

Spending the day sitting in a prickly tree didn't appeal to me. Everything went quiet, and I considered my options. First I tasted one of the red berries that hung there, and it was disgusting. A cat could get hungry and uncomfortable stuck up here all day. I longed for the lovely home we had left, and I was full of sadness.

Ellen was calling me, and banging our cat food dish with a spoon, like she always did when she wanted to get our attention. Eventually I wormed my way down and crawled on my belly along the base of the wall, following a tunnel that some other creature had conveniently made through the long grasses. When I finally reached the caravan, the door was open and I bounded in with my tail up again.

Jessica was back and she was setting up a place for herself inside the cupboard under the seats. She'd already got a dead mouse in there, and one of Ellen's socks, and a Dairylea cheese portion. She was pleased to see me for once.

'Poof,' she said when I told her about the dog. 'I can sort him out. Don't be such a wimp, Solomon.'

'You haven't seen how big he is,' I said.

'Poof,' Jessica yawned contemptuously. 'Dogs are nothing to me.'

We spread ourselves out on the sunny windowsill to sleep. It wasn't peaceful in the caravan with John bouncing on and off the seats and throwing his toys around. Joe was on the steps drilling holes in the door, fitting a puss flap for us, and Ellen was getting more and more stressed as she tried to unpack boxes. I looked guiltily at the red scratches on her shoulder. She'd forgiven me, but I still felt bad. And Jessica had called me a wimp.

Soon Joe was shouting at John, and getting angry with the caravan door. He'd made a hole in it, and taken the new puss flap out of its box, only to find it didn't fit.

I watched him tensely as he struggled with it. Then he flung it under the caravan.

'Useless rubbish,' he complained, and threw his whole toolbox outside. It clattered onto the grass, screws and nails bouncing everywhere.

Jessica disappeared into her cupboard, and John ran to Ellen, clinging round her legs. Ellen's face went tight. I knew she didn't dare to speak at times like this. Anything she said, even kind things, would send Joe into a frenzy. Trapped on the windowsill, I half closed my eyes and pretended to be a Buddha, setting an example of how to be peaceful.

With John now clinging round her neck, Ellen opened the fridge and took out one of the tall black and gold cans of beer that Joe liked. She handed it to him silently. He took it, and leaned on the car with his back to everyone.

'Come on, we need some time outside.' Ellen carried John down the steps and dragged his plastic tractor out from under the caravan. I followed them with my tail up and sat on the path, which was warm and dry, while John pedalled up and down.

And then the dog appeared. It was ambling down the path, all by itself. It hadn't seen us yet. I froze, knowing that if I even twitched, it would see me and charge, putting John and Ellen in danger too.

Jessica seemed to have some sort of radar. She came out immediately, running low in the grass like a stalking tiger. I could feel the heat of her as she swept past me. She sat down in the middle of the path, and started washing. Her audacity was breathtaking. The dog ambled nearer and nearer, but Jessica went on washing.

I wanted to run, but how could I leave Jessica, John and Ellen to face that dog?

Suddenly it looked up, saw us and charged down the path, its paws rattling on the tarmac.

Jessica stood up and transformed herself into a dragon. She arched her back, flattened her ears, blackened her eyes and lashed her tail. Her fur bristled until she was twice her usual size. She stepped towards the dog, her mouth open showing an array of ferocious little fangs, and she yowled and growled.

'Mummy, look at Jessica!' squeaked John, and we all stood like statues, watching.

The dog stopped barking. It hesitated, then slouched up to Jessica, snuffling and snorting, its glinty eyes fixed on her. She looked so small, like a toy cat against the massive bulk of the dog. Still she inched towards it, glaring and spitting. Then she sprang forward and lashed out with a long paw. Her claws flashed in the sunshine as she caught the dog right on its sensitive nose.

It yelped and backed away, rubbing its hurt nose with big soft paws. Not content with one slash, Jessica flew at the dog and boxed its ears. It fled, yelping and whimpering, back up the path, its tail tucked in and its ears flapping.

John and Ellen, and even Joe cheered and clapped Jessica.

'What a gutsy little cat!'

But Jessica wasn't interested in accolades. She sat down again and resumed washing as if nothing had happened.

Later on, the little man with the purple aura came walking down, without the dog. Ellen gave him a mug of hot tea and he sat in the caravan slurping it and apologising.

'He wasn't meant to be out. Some idiot left the gate open,' he explained. 'He's a rescue dog. Daft as a brush he is, daft as a brush. And he's all I've got since my wife died.'

I walked along the seat and stepped carefully onto his lap, looking up at him. His name was Nick, and his scratchy old coat smelt of dog, but I tried not to mind as I rubbed and purred. Nick was horrible, and so was his dog, but I could see the loneliness in his eyes. I spread myself out, stretching my long paws over his heart.

'What a beautiful cat,' Nick said. 'He's got a shine on him, and so friendly. Daft as a brush.'

'That's Solomon,' explained Ellen. 'And he's a big softie.'

After Nick had gone, Ellen picked me up and cuddled me.

'You've done something really important, Solomon,' she said. 'Nick is the campsite owner and we've got to stay friends with him. Otherwise he could chuck us out.'

I felt proud. I was a healing cat. What I did was just as important as Jessica's moment of glory. I loved her for her courageous performance with the dog. She was a star and she'd been given a whole tin of sardines to herself.

After that encounter, the dog, whose name was Paisley, would not come anywhere near us. When Nick took him out on the long lead, Paisley made a wide circle around our caravan, and Jessica would magically appear and sit on the steps ostentatiously washing, just to wind him up. Paisley never barked at me again, or at John. We were part of Queen Jessica's domain.

Pam-next-door soon became a friend. She had a dog, if you could call it a dog. It was smaller than Jessica and had legs like a fairy, and ears like wings. Pam dressed it up in tartan coats and put bows in its hair, and it travelled around in the basket of the shiny white bike she rode out on every day, pedalling vigorously.

Pam didn't like Joe. She would only come in if he wasn't there, and when he talked to her she looked at him sceptically as if she knew his darkest secrets.

Joe never did finish fitting the puss flap. It stayed under the caravan where he had chucked it, and there was just a square hole in the door. As autumn turned to winter, the wind and rain howled through the hole and it was freezing in the caravan. At night Ellen wedged a cushion against it, and Jessica and I learned to push it aside when we wanted to go out.

On windy nights it was scary inside the caravan. It rocked and trembled, and the sycamore trees flung broken twigs and branches down onto the roof. It was so alarming that I felt the need to find a refuge somewhere outside; a dry safe hole where Jessica and I could go, even in the night. So I spent long hours exploring on my own.

I walked up and down the lane that ran past the campsite. I made friends with people who walked along it, especially a girl with long dark hair. She told me her name was Karenza, and she always stopped to stroke me. One day she picked me up and we had a real bonding session, touching noses and rubbing each other's faces. Sometimes I followed Karenza home and peeped at her cottage, which was a long way down the lane. She had cats. They were always on the wall or round the cottage door, or sometimes sitting in the window looking fat and contented. Lucky cats. Karenza's cottage was top of my list of refuges.

One moonlit night I climbed over the hedge and into the sycamore copse. I wanted to explore the deep dark holes I'd seen, and find out who lived in them. First I climbed several different trees, some of them quite high, and established comfortable perches – places I could run to quickly if necessary. I had a mad half hour there on my own and practised some high-speed manoeuvres up and down my chosen trees, my paws dashing through the dry sycamore leaves with a spectacular rustling.

Then I heard something moving, sensed it, smelled it. From the safety of my tree, I watched black and white creatures come shuffling out of the holes. They had pointed faces with a white stripe that shone in the moonlight. They were quiet, snuffly animals with wise black eyes and a cloud of fur like thistledown. Badgers.

Carefully I slid down from the tree. I wanted to meet a badger. I wanted to see inside one of those big holes. I wanted to know if a cat like me would be welcome to shelter there in an emergency.

At first the badgers were snorty and aggressive with me and I had to keep jumping into trees to get out of their way. It took weeks of patient hanging around, purring and pretending to be asleep before I gained the privilege of a nose-to-nose hello with the oldest and wisest badger. I wasn't allowed into their holes, but one night the old badger led me along the base of the stone hedge and showed me a hole which they had made and abandoned. It was perfect. Lined with moss and cosy dry grass, facing south, and big enough for two cats to curl up and sleep.

That winter night I was glad I'd found a refuge. As I trotted home through the sycamore copse I heard an old familiar sound coming from the caravan.

Shouting and screaming.

CHAPTER SIX

GOING TO THE VET

The caravan door crashed open and Jessica came flying out. Ellen was screaming at Joe.

'Don't hurt Jessica! If you touch her I'll …'

'You'll what?'

Joe loomed in the doorway like a thunderstorm, his car keys jingling in his hand. Jessica had dived into the hedge, a huge chicken leg in her mouth. A plate came whizzing out after her, with peas and potatoes bouncing onto the grass. I loved roast potatoes, so I made a note of where they landed as I watched from one of my safe perches.

'If you'd come in for your supper when I called you, it wouldn't have happened, Joe,' Ellen said. 'It's natural for a cat to want to grab food they like the look of. And you should know that. I'm not cooking for you if you're too busy drinking to turn up.'

'Lecture, lecture, lecture!' Joe mocked. 'That's all you ever do now.'

'And look how you've wasted that food, Joe. We can't AFFORD decent food very often.' Ellen couldn't seem to stop yelling. She was close to tears. 'Chucking good food away is an abuse of the whole of creation.'

'Oh, so that's why you sat there and let the cat nick my supper. Or is that my fault as well? Blame Joe. That's what you always do. I'm going to the pub to get a pasty, where I'm going to sit and eat it without some cow nagging me.'

'But you can't drive, Joe. You've been drinking.'

'Just watch me.' Joe got in the car and revved it. A cloud of stinking smoke came out of the exhaust. 'And who cares if I don't come back? Some home this is.'

'It's your fault we lost our lovely house,' cried Ellen and she bent over, clutching her stomach as Joe drove off. 'That place was special to me. It was my mum's home. She planted the cherry tree and I played under it when I was a child. I miss it all so much.' Then she crept into the caravan as if the pain of her words was breaking her in half.

I waited until Joe's car had gone squealing out of the campsite. I listened, and I could hear Jessica rustling and growling as she ate her stolen dinner under the hedge. From the caravan came the sound of Ellen trying to comfort John, and the clink of plates being stacked. I was anxious. I wanted to go straight in there and do my job with the healing stars and the purring, but I was finding it increasingly difficult to go into the caravan. It was cramped and smelly now. John's toys were everywhere, and my sunny windowsill was often covered in damp washing, so there was nowhere for me to sit.

It was nearly dark and the sky was an ominous glassy purple. A storm was brewing and I didn't want to be inside that shuddering caravan. I felt guilty too. My job as a cat was to look after Ellen, and I wasn't doing it. Nothing was the same.

Before we moved into the caravan, the rows between Joe and Ellen had been stormy but brief. Joe had usually come back sorry and ashamed with a bunch of flowers or a box of cream cakes. He'd sit on the sofa with Ellen cuddled up to him and they'd talk far into the night. Joe did most of the talking, trying to explain how guilty he felt and why he lost his temper, and Ellen always forgave him. Jessica and I used to bask in the healing atmosphere, both of us purring, happy cats on the warm sofa where there was plenty of room for all of us. Two cats on two laps, and John falling asleep nestled in between his mum and dad.

But now the rows went on and on, and there were no apologies, no flowers and no cream cakes. Joe resented living in the caravan, and that night when he came back from the pub, instead of sitting up with Ellen, he stomped off to bed and slammed the door. Ellen popped outside to call Jessica who was out there somewhere in the cold, too frightened to come in. Then she sat with us on her lap, and I could feel the sadness in her heart.

'I had a cat just like you, Solomon,' she told me as I stretched my paws over her thin shoulders, and Jessica lay there playfully patting the wispy ends of Ellen's hair. 'When I was a child. He was called Solomon too, and he used to run down the road to meet me from school. I read him stories and played him music on the piano.' Her voice broke into a sob. 'Oh I wish we still had my piano. I miss it so much. And Joe is so angry.'

That night she slept on the long caravan seat with a rug over her, and we snuggled in there with her. I stayed awake, worrying about what Joe was going to do in the morning.

'What's wrong with him?' I asked my angel, and she went into one of her silences.

'He's in prison,' she said eventually.

'Prison?' I knew what prison was. A cat cage for humans.

'It's a prison made of anger,' said my angel. 'He's made it himself and he's keeping the door locked. No one has sent him there.'

I pondered on these words while rain pounded on the roof. I remembered the badgers out in the copse and wondered what it would be like to be wild. Just before dawn, the rain stopped and orange sunshine filtered through wet branches. Ellen and John got up quietly. No one wanted to wake Joe. The row they'd had was still alive, a grumpy troll lurking under a bridge, like the one in John's favourite story. It was called *Billy Goats Gruff*, and I'd heard it lots of times. Now I felt we were all tiptoeing over that scary bridge, and the tiniest creak would rouse the sleeping troll.

After such a rough night, Jessica and I were glad to stretch out side by side on the sunny windowsill, and I drifted into a deep sleep until mid-morning. A loud thump woke me, and the caravan shuddered. A cup fell off the table and rolled across the floor. I heard Ellen shouting.

'You're not having the car keys, Joe. You're drunk.'

There was a chilling sound of glass smashing and peppering down like hailstones, and John started to cry. Then the caravan shook again. Thump, thump, thump. The troll was awake.

We two cats sprang to life and bolted outside, straight under the hedge. Those first weeks had taught us that the caravan was not a safe place. The only haven for us was outside in one of our hiding places. We crouched under the bracken next to one another and Jessica suddenly did something very sweet. She stretched her cute little face to me and touched noses. I kissed her back and our white whiskers brushed together.

It made me feel a whole lot better.

'It'll be OK,' she said. 'Let them get on with it. We've got each other haven't we?'

I gave her a special purr-meow.

Then we huddled together and listened.

'What is the matter with you, Joe? You never used to be like this.' Ellen was clutching the car keys in her hand. 'And how did this car window get smashed? Tell me.'

Joe was leaning on the car, with one hand pushed into his ginger hair. His eyes were tightly shut, and clenched in his other hand was a hammer.

'Go to your room, John and stay there please,' said Ellen, steering John up the steps and into the caravan. '*Please* sweetheart. Mummy will sort this out.'

'Daddy kicked the caravan.' John wailed. 'It's not safe in there, Mummy. Daddy was going to knock it over.'

'No he wasn't. Just go to your room, John.'

'NO!'

John ran round behind the caravan and lay on the ground sobbing.

'Do as you're told,' roared Joe, and in a few angry strides he had grabbed John, pushed him inside the caravan and shut the door. Joe leaned against it, breathing hard and looking at Ellen with pain in his eyes. 'Don't go running after him. Let him cry for once. It's ME you should start caring about.'

'I do care about you, Joe,' said Ellen. 'But you're getting worse and worse. I can't cope with you being so angry.'

Joe picked up the hammer from where he had

dropped it. 'This is what damaged your precious car. I bloody smashed it. And why? 'Cause YOU refused to give me the keys. So I smashed the window. How else was I supposed to get in?'

'You're upsetting John,' said Ellen. 'And me. And the cats. If you don't stop it we'll get thrown off this camp-site, Joe.'

'See this?' Joe held up the hammer, and Ellen went pale. 'This is what you'll get if you don't SHUT UP nagging me every five minutes. *Stop drinking Joe. Get a job Joe.* That's all you ever say to me now. I'm sick, sick, SICK of it, woman!'

He began to pace to and fro, brandishing the hammer. It glinted in the sun and so did his eyes. Ellen pressed her back against the caravan, her aura flaming with fear and anger. She tried to say something and Joe immediately went into a new frenzy.

'You say two words and I'll put this hammer straight through that windscreen.'

Sitting under the hedge, Jessica and I peered out through the bracken fronds. 'Don't let him hurt my Ellen,' I was praying. I hoped Ellen would keep quiet and let Joe calm down, and she did. 'Please send an angel. Please,' I prayed, and at that moment the door of Pam's caravan opened, and Pam came bustling over.

'Nosy old crow,' muttered Joe, and he flung the hammer under the caravan.

Goodness knows what might have happened if Pam hadn't come. She had her shoulders square and her chin in the air, and she was smiling!

'Hello Joe. Doing some DIY are you?' she quipped. 'Eee – how did that car window get smashed? What a shame. Have to mend it now won't you? Expensive aren't they, cars? I'm glad I've only got me bike. Now, how would you like to come and have a coffee, Ellen? Bring John. I've just made some gingerbread. Do you want to come, Joe?'

Joe glared at Pam. 'No thanks.' He turned and walked off, his hands in his pockets, and we watched him turn out of the gate and head up the road. Pam had done a better job than any angel, I thought.

Nothing was easy and fun like it had been in our lovely house. I longed to go back there, and often I sat gazing at the distant road curving around the hill. That was the road home. But every time I did this, my angel told me I had to stay here.

She arrived in a blaze of stars a couple of days later as I crouched on the wide mossy branch of a tree.

'Wait, Solomon,' she said. 'Don't go into the caravan just yet.'

So I sat patiently in the tree, listening to the first gusts of autumn wind scattering the dry leaves. My angel's voice was easy to hear, like the twang of a bell in my head, but when I tried to see her in detail she was screened by a shining mist. Mostly I sensed her energy ruffling my fur, and her voice clearing my mind. I appreciated this, as it needed clearing out. My mind was full of homesickness and anxiety. Even anger was in there sometimes, and my angel would sweep it all out as if she had a brush made of stardust. I always felt better once it had been swept away.

Someone in a billowing raincoat was walking towards the caravan in the twilight, a small torchlight bobbing in her hand. It was Pam. But looking closer, I sat up in amazement. Floating beside her was a lady in a glistening, shimmering robe, a lady with a radiant smile and loving eyes. Ellen's mum. Now I knew why the angel had told me to wait.

Overjoyed to see the visitor from the spirit world, I meowed, leapt down from the tree and dashed across the grass. For the first time that day, my tail was up straight as I ran to her. Ellen's mum was guiding Pam-next-door towards the caravan, but she paused to whisper some loving words to me.

'Hello Solomon. You are a darling cat. You're doing a wonderful, wonderful job. Thank you.'

She brushed her warm hands over my fur and suddenly I felt better. Her praise encouraged me and I flexed my back and purred, rubbing against Pam's legs. She bent down and picked me up.

'Eee, you're a lovely cat you are.'

Cuddling me with one arm, Pam knocked on the caravan window. I realised that Pam couldn't see Ellen's mum, who quickly disappeared when Ellen opened the door.

Settling on Ellen's lap, I could still feel the love of her mum's smile, and my purring was deep and soothing. Ellen stroked me with one hand and John's hair with the other as he leaned against her on the long caravan seat, his face still dirty from crying.

'Is John asleep?' Pam whispered, sitting herself down on the seat opposite.

'Yes. He's out for the count, Pam, you needn't whisper,' said Ellen. Her voice sounded wobbly.

'I came to see if you were all right.' Pam's eyes were full of kindness. 'I heard Joe go off like that in the car. I couldn't help hearing the row.'

Ellen started to cry. She cried and cried, and Pam just sat there offering her tissues out of a box, and making motherly comments like, 'Oh dear. Oh dear, oh dear. Oh you poor girl.'

'I hate it here in this caravan. I can't cope with being here, Pam. We lost our home you see – they repossessed it. It was my mum's home and she left it to me, but Joe got into debt and mortgaged it. They took all our furniture, they even took my piano. If Nick hadn't let us in here we'd be homeless. I thought we'd try and make the best of it but it's getting worse and worse, Pam, especially with – now that Joe is …' Her voice came to a halt. She couldn't speak. I stretched out my paws and lay over her heart, my chin on her chest. She felt bony and thin and her inner light was very very dim as if it was about to go out.

'Joe's on benefits,' said Ellen. 'We both tried to get jobs, but there just aren't any here in Cornwall. They keep telling us there will be jobs in the spring when the tourist season starts, but how can we survive until then?'

'He's drinking isn't he?' asked Pam, and a new wave of pain seemed to engulf Ellen and came pouring out in a deluge of words and tears, her whole body shaking and sobbing.

'I know,' Pam went on. 'I don't miss much. Anyway, you can smell it on him. How's he going to get home?'

'I don't know, Pam.' Ellen shook her head. 'He'll have to walk. Sometimes he stays out all night. Oh Pam, I'm so frightened. If he goes on like this, Nick will chuck us off the site. Then where will we go? We've got nowhere to go, Pam, nowhere.'

Pam leaned forward and made Ellen look at her courageous blue eyes. 'I won't let him,' she declared. 'And you can come in with me any time. You remember that. I'll be like a – a mum to you, and I'll be a granny for John. I love him, and you, and this beautiful cat.'

'We've got no money,' Ellen wept. 'It all goes on Joe's booze and the rent.'

Pam shook her fist. 'He's got to be stopped.'

'No Pam, don't you get involved,' said Ellen, but I knew that Pam would. I could see that Pam was like Jessica – gutsy and brave, even if she was an old lady. She was going to have a go at Joe. I couldn't wait.

'He used to be a lovely man,' said Ellen. 'He was over the moon when John was born.'

Pam got up and made two mugs of steaming cocoa. Then she rummaged in the cupboard and found a tin of Whiskas rabbit, my favourite. I jumped down to eat it, and I got a compliment as well.

'This cat, Solomon, he's special,' Pam said, stroking my back as I tucked in. 'He's the most beautiful, loving cat I've ever seen. He's trying to look after you, Ellen. Don't you ever let him go will you? He's heaven sent, this cat.'

After that, I felt so much better that I settled down in the caravan with Ellen and John. Joe didn't come back, and despite the wild storm outside, we had a night of peace. Jessica came slinking back through the hole in the door and we curled up together on the amber velvet cushion.

We survived the rest of the winter. Joe came and went, losing his temper and apologising, then he'd try to be nice for a few days. It never lasted.

As spring turned to summer, life seemed easier. John

was growing fast and running around the campsite with other children. Ellen had the washing outside in the sun, and even a few pots of flowers. While Joe spent whole mornings lying in bed, Ellen was cleaning and polishing and keeping John happy. Jessica and I had a bit of fun, chasing each other up and down trees. She liked to go up to Nick's house and tease Paisley by sitting on top of the gatepost. The poor dog would shiver and shake, and if Jessica jumped down into his garden, he would bolt indoors, yelping.

I showed Jessica all my refuges, including the badger hole, and we had a few experimental naps in it. She wouldn't come down the road with me to visit Karenza's cottage, so I went alone and socialised with her cats. I kept friends with the badgers too, it was part of my plan to build a support network to help me in times of trouble.

One hot summer day, after a wild chase through the copse with Jessica, I got a prickle stuck in my paw. I licked and fussed but it wouldn't come out, and days later it turned into an abscess. My paw was swollen and throbbing painfully. It was full of poison. Miserably, I crouched in the shade underneath the caravan. I didn't want to eat or move.

Ellen kept picking me up and holding my bad paw in a basin of hot salty water. It was comforting, but soon I felt so ill I just crawled deeper under the caravan and sat there, shivering.

'I'll have to take you to the vet, Solomon.' Ellen wriggled under the caravan on her tummy to get me out. I lay in her arms, all floppy like a dead cat.

'Get the cat basket, Joe,' she said. 'I'm taking Solomon in right now. He's really sick.'

'We can't afford vet's fees, Ellen.'

'I don't care. I'm taking him.'

'And who's going to pay for it?'

Ellen didn't answer. She put me down and dragged the cat basket out of its cupboard. Within minutes she and Joe were arguing while I lay there with a headache.

'I am not letting Solomon die because of your self-ishness,' Ellen said angrily. 'What's the matter with you, Joe?'

She put me into the cat basket. I felt so ill that I didn't much care whether I lived or died. It would be OK to die. I could go home to the spirit world, to the lovely valley with the cushiony grass. An easy option. But Ellen would be left here with all the problems. I hadn't done my work. So I lay there, struggling to stay alive, my paw hot and throbbing.

Ellen was fighting to hang on to the car keys, which Joe was trying to prise out of her hands, and John was clinging to Ellen's sleeve.

'Please let me come, Mummy. I don't want to stay with Daddy.' He started to scream. 'Mummy, *please*.'

'Shut up.' Joe pushed John and he fell backwards out

of the caravan. John got up slowly, rubbing his elbow
and howling.

'Oh, sorry son. I didn't mean you to fall.' Joe was
suddenly quiet again, shamefaced. But the shadow of his
temper was still there. I watched it sadly through half-
closed eyes, feeling powerless and very sick. I opened
my mouth and managed a really loud meow, more like
a cry, and even though he was hurt, little John came and
pressed his hot face against the bars of the cat basket.

'Poor Solomon,' he cried. 'I love you, Solomon. I'm
coming with you and I won't let that vet hurt you.'

Even in my comatose state I looked into John's eyes
and saw the beautiful caring soul that was in there. The
whole child was shining in an aura of golden light. I
managed to reach out a good paw and pat him gently
through the bars, feeling encouraged. I'd found another
friend who loved me.

Ellen and Joe were looking at each other silently.
One small loving gesture from John had turned into a
golden moment of healing that wrapped itself around
the troubled family.

'I'll drive,' said Joe quietly. 'I'll be really careful, I
promise.'

I was too ill to feel frightened. I just lay in the cat
basket, my chin on the amber velvet cushion, and I felt
more at peace. Little John had done my work for me.
Now he sat beside me in his car seat, talking to me,

telling me how he was going to grow up and be a vet and heal animals.

All three of them came into the surgery with me, and I was grateful for their presence as I lay limply on the cold steel table.

This vet was a pretty dark-eyed woman called Abby. She examined me gently and spoke softly to me.

'He's very ill,' she explained. 'He needs an immediate shot of antibiotics which I'll give him now.'

John went on stroking my head with his small hand while Abby gave me some injections.

'You are a good lad,' she said to John. 'I could do with a helper like you.'

'And I've got a bad elbow,' John said. 'I fell out of the caravan. But I stopped crying for Solomon's sake 'cause he's got a sore paw.'

Ellen and Joe stood close, just looking at each other and holding hands. Ellen was very pale and still had tears on her cheeks.

'This stuff is a painkiller,' explained Abby, giving me a second injection. 'You're being such a good cat, Solomon. I wish they were all like you.'

Then she did something to my paw, cutting the abscess, and I could feel the hot pain draining away. I felt suddenly sleepy and soft.

'He's purring. Mummy, he's purring,' said John.

'He knows he's being made better,' I heard Ellen say

as I drifted off, and Abby's words were even more distant.

'Keep him warm and quiet. Give him one of these tablets every six hours and make sure he swallows it. He's a young strong cat and he should get better.'

I woke up in the caravan on Ellen's lap. She was stroking me softly as if I was made of gossamer, and her hands were warm and full of stardust. It was so lovely, I pretended to be asleep again, floating and drifting, and in my dream I heard music. I remembered my past life as Ellen's cat, how we had danced on the lawn, and the times when I had sat on top of the piano while she played music that tingled in my bones. What had happened to make Ellen change so much? I asked my angel.

'Life has happened,' she said.

'So why have I been ill?' I asked.

'It's a gift,' said my angel.

'A gift?'

'Sometimes illness is a gift. It gives you a time to heal in body and soul. It's like a spiritual holiday. And it calms and strengthens the people who have to look after you, it reminds them how to be kind. It's a blessing in disguise.'

I understood. I would rest and get better now, and let Ellen pamper me. But even as I lay there pretending to sleep, I kept one eye on Joe. He was sprawled in a corner, drinking can after can of beer and chucking the empty ones on the caravan floor.

The next minute Nick was standing at the open caravan door, looking very serious.

'Been drinking again, have you Joe?' He looked into the caravan at the piles of empty cans. 'I've come to collect your rent. Have you got it?'

Joe stood up. I felt Ellen's hands go stiff. What was going to happen now?

CHAPTER
SEVEN

'YOU CHEEKY CAT'

John started school that autumn. Ellen took him every morning in the car. She started staying out for a long time, and we cats were left alone with Joe. The first thing Joe did was to pull Jessica out of her basket, holding her roughly with one hand under her tummy. Even if it was raining he dumped her outside, clapped his hands and shooed her away. One day he did the same to me. I felt so hurt. I turned around and looked at him reproachfully, flicking my tail, but he slammed the door. Clearly he didn't want us.

Jessica was catching mice in the hedge. She stashed them under the caravan and waited for her chance to sneak one inside and into her private cupboard. I headed down the lane to Karenza's cottage, the chilly wind ruffling my fur. Jessica and I were hungry. Our food was getting less and less, and we relied on mice or the little treats Pam gave us more than ever. Today one of Karenza's cats, a big ginger tom, kindly shared his dish with me. He had plenty so I ate as much as I could. Karenza opened her door and I peered in, tempted by the warmth of her cosy stove. I wanted to go in and curl up on the rug with the cats who were already there.

'Hello Solomon,' Karenza said brightly. 'Oh yes, I know your name. Your Ellen's been telling me all about you, what a special cat you are.' She picked me up and gave me a cuddle, and I leaned on her, soaking up her warmth and cheerfulness. I thought she was going to carry me inside and let me sit by the fire, but she put me down again. 'You go home, Solomon,' she said as I rubbed myself against the black boots she always wore, and she guided me firmly outside and shut the door.

Disappointed, I sat down on the doorstep to think. The easy days of summer had passed, and soon we faced another winter. The morning sky was yellow and grey, the wind zigzagged up the lane, stripping leaves from the sycamores. Above me on the telephone wires, a crowd of swallows had gathered, twittering and fussing. I watched them fly away to the south and I knew they were going to a better warmer place thousands of miles away. I wished I was a swallow instead of a cat.

My angel was twinkling at me urgently.

'Go home,' she said. 'Quickly.'

I hurried up the lane, dashed across the copse and over the hedge to the caravan, a feeling of dread in my throat. What had happened now? I soon knew.

Ellen was sitting doubled up with pain, a basin in her hand. Her face was yellowish white and frightened. Pam was sitting one side of her and Joe the other.

'You've got to go to hospital, Ellen,' Pam was saying, her arm around Ellen's tense shoulders, and Ellen was shaking her head.

'No. No, Pam. I can't be ill. What about John, and the cats?'

'I'll take care of John,' Pam said warmly.

'And I can manage the cats for goodness' sake,' said Joe.

Ellen just looked at him hopelessly.

I ran to her and jumped on her lap.

'Get out cat,' Joe tried to push me aside.

'Don't call him cat,' cried Ellen. 'This is SOLOMON. Let him stay.'

I glared at Joe and settled on the seat as close to Ellen as I could get. She was doubled over with pain and her body felt stiff.

Joe stood up and took the car keys from their hook.

'I'm taking you to hospital right now.'

'How much have you had to drink?' asked Pam sharply.

'Nothing today, promise. I never drink until after lunch.'

Pam looked at Ellen and raised her eyebrows.

'Is that true?'

'Course it's true. I'm not a liar.'

'Don't you raise your voice at me, Joe.' Pam's eyes

flared at Joe. 'I'm going to be looking after John. I'll fetch him from school on me bike and I'll clean up for you too, so don't get lippy with me.'

Ellen looked too ill to care what happened. I stared deep into her eyes, trying to tell her I loved her. Then I kissed her on the nose, purring and purring. She took my face in both hands.

'Thank you for being my cat, Solomon,' she said. 'Now you stay here, and Jessica too, and Joe will bring me back when I'm better.'

Joe picked her up and carried her out to the car while Pam bustled around stuffing things into a bag: Ellen's slippers, her hairbrush and wash bag. She took down a photo frame with a picture of John holding me and smiling, and popped that in. When I heard the bag being zipped up and the car starting I felt uneasy. I ran to sit on the steps, and as the car drove off Ellen looked back at me.

In that moment of parting, I felt so close to Ellen. We had shared so much. Joe saw Ellen as a tired woman with haunted eyes endlessly shrieking at him, often frowning as she tried to cope. Only I knew the bright, creative soul of Ellen, the child with honey gold hair and passion in her eyes, who cared about tiny birds and animals, who only wanted to play beautiful music and dance in the wind. In that earlier lifetime she'd given me so much love and fun. It tore me apart to watch her being driven away to a place where I couldn't reach her.

Jessica crept out of her cupboard and we both sat on the windowsill, watching Pam cleaning up the caravan. She worked energetically, gathering Joe's empty beer cans into a bag, stacking his motoring magazines, washing up and folding clothes. She tutted and grumbled, and talked non-stop.

'He's a lazy so and so, that Joe. He doesn't deserve a lovely wife like Ellen, and two beautiful cats like you. Now you cats have got to be good.' Pam turned and wagged her finger at us. 'You've got to be good quiet cats and keep out of his way. I'll have John in with me, but I can't have you two in my caravan because of me dog. Have you got that, Jessica?'

Jessica's buttercup eyes sparkled at Pam as if they shared a private joke.

'And don't you shred his precious magazines.' Pam pointed her finger at Jessica who was enjoying the attention. 'And don't bring mice in. He hates that. You just be good quiet cats and I'll keep an eye on you till Ellen gets back, poor girl. She's gone to hospital, and that's like you going to the vet. Not fun, but they'll make her better, you'll see.'

Pam sounded confident and reassuring. I was glad to have her there. She seemed like an earth angel to me. When she'd gone to fetch John, Jessica and I settled down for a long sleep with the afternoon sun streaming through the window onto our fur.

At dusk I sat on the caravan steps, waiting for Ellen to return. Paisley was ambling along the hedge on his own. He paused and looked at me, one paw in the air. I didn't move. I knew that Jessica would come out, puffed up like a porcupine, if Paisley dared to approach. I still didn't fancy tackling him on my own though.

I could hear the badgers coming out of their hole, and the magpies chattering as they went home to roost. I listened to every car that came down the lane, and finally I heard the familiar rattle of Joe's car and the squeal of tyres as he braked and turned into the campsite. Paisley's eyes shone red in the headlight.

'Daddy, Daddy.' John came running. 'I had tea with Pam. And she's given me a cake for Mummy.'

He flung himself at the car window, the cake in his hand. It looked nice. A fruit bun with a cherry on top.

But the passenger seat was empty.

Ellen wasn't there.

Joe heaved himself out of the car and locked it. He squatted down to talk to John.

'Mummy's very sick,' he said. 'She's got to stay in hospital for a long time.'

John stared at him, his face crumpling. Then he squashed the cake in his hand, hurled it under the caravan, and ran away into the darkness.

'Get back here NOW,' shouted Joe, but John ignored him.

I understood what Joe had said about Ellen. It shocked me. How would we all live without Ellen? How could I be her cat if she wasn't there? I made up my mind to go and find her.

Jessica dived under the caravan and seized the cake. She reversed into the dark with it, growling, and sat there picking off the crinkly paper.

'Thieving, opportunist moggy.' Joe slammed into the caravan and I heard him opening the fridge and taking out beer cans.

I ran after John. Like me, he had refuges where he could hide if he needed to, and I knew where most of them were. I found him sitting on a pile of pallets round the back of Nick's place, and to my surprise Paisley was leaning against John's legs, his big chin on the boy's knee. He was being very loving, offering John his huge paw, and John was talking to him. It changed my attitude to dogs. Obviously John had made friends with Paisley when I wasn't around. There were even a few healing stars drifting around the two of them, and Paisley was so intent on comforting John that he didn't even glance in my direction. I was glad that John had a friend, it left me free to go and find Ellen.

'You can't do that,' Jessica said, when I told her my plans.

'Why not?'

'You could get lost, or run over by a car,' she said.

'And I don't fancy living here alone with Joe.'

'You can have my badger hole,' I offered, but Jessica pooh-poohed that idea.

'I'm a carpet cat. I don't *do* badger holes,' she said, washing her pink paws vigorously. 'I dream of living with a little old lady who will pamper me when my work is done.'

'Not if you shred magazines.'

'I shan't do it. I shall be a model cat,' said Jessica haughtily.

'I'll miss you,' I said, and Jessica came and made a fuss of me, licking my ears and my back, purring her funny little purr.

'So what is your work?' I asked.

Jessica thought for a moment. 'Loving you.' Then she said sadly, 'And our kittens. I still miss them. My two boys, and the little tabby girl. Our little girl loved you very much didn't she?'

'I loved her,' I said, 'and I wonder where she is now.'

'Perhaps we'll never know.' Jessica's eyes went dark and I realised then how much the kittens had meant to her, and why she had cried all the way to Cornwall. Although Jessica was a tough cat, she too felt a mother's grief.

I was a smart cat. I did a lot of thinking before deciding how best to find Ellen. After my long trip in the lorry as a kitten, I had a deep fear of travelling. I spent some time making friends with Joe's car, sitting on it when it was warm, and sneaking inside if I got the chance. I scent-marked the tyres so that it would be easy for me to find.

It soon became obvious that Joe went to visit Ellen in the afternoons while Pam looked after John. Sometimes he had a few flowers or a bag of fruit. He was always gone for about three hours, and when he came back he just sat in the caravan drinking and sleeping.

I sensed Ellen's direction. She was north-east of the campsite, and not too far away if I headed straight across the fields.

'No, Solomon,' said my angel. 'You would come to the city and you'd get lost. That would worry Ellen. The only way is to be really brave and go in Joe's car. He'll take you, and bring you back, but you mustn't look frightened. Keep a bright face and hold your tail high, and you will get there.'

So one morning when the car doors were open I crept inside and made a nest underneath a coat on the back seat. It was a scary thing for a cat to do, but I kept quiet and still as Joe started the engine and drove off.

We were speeding along the roads, twisting and turning, going uphill and down. I longed to look out of the window and see landmarks to help me find the way home, but I stayed hidden. If Joe saw me he might lose his temper. My angel had warned me.

'You're taking on a difficult challenge, Solomon,' she'd said. 'Cats can't normally go into hospitals. I'll be surprised if you do manage this, but if Joe sees you, you've got no chance, so lie low, and when he arrives you must jump out immediately.'

When the car slowed down, I figured we were arriving, and I peeped out from under the coat. The hospital was a block of concrete towering into the sky, its windows winking in the sun. Around it were green lawns and interesting trees where I could hide.

Joe opened the door to get out, and I was crouched, waiting. I slithered out like a snake, past his leg and under the car. I watched his feet in the old grey and black trainers he wore, and the ragged edge of his jeans, and when I saw them walking away, I followed.

'Don't look furtive,' said my angel. 'Put your tail up and look as if you've every right to be here.'

So I did. Joe never looked back and I strutted after him through the car park and along a wide path that curved under the big trees. Autumn leaves were dancing everywhere and I longed to play with them, but I focused on following Joe.

People started noticing me and calling me 'Puss' and 'That Cat', but I trotted on, my head and tail high, right through the glass doors and into the echoing hospital. I was going to see Ellen.

'WHAT is THAT CAT doing in here?'

'Who let THAT CAT in?'

It was hard to keep going with sharp-voiced comments bouncing around me. Luckily there were compliments too.

'Aw. Look at that gorgeous cat.'

'He knows where he's going. He must live here.'

I was proud of myself – parading along the corridors with everyone smiling at me. I stiffened my whiskers and stuck my chin in the air. I imagined my coat was gleaming like black silk and that I, Solomon, was the King of cats. Ellen wouldn't want a frightened, creeping cat, she would want King Solomon in all his glory.

Still Joe didn't look round. Oblivious of his surroundings, he strode on through the hospital. Turning left, he headed up the stairs, two steps at a time. His aura was bright so I guessed we must be getting close to Ellen. I so wanted to meow.

Left again and down a long pale green corridor, my paws skidding on the polished floor. I wished Jessica was there. What a game we could have had, galloping and sliding and making people laugh. Playing penguins.

At the end of the corridor was a wide doorway into a bright room full of high beds. A nurse with a fierce face popped out of a side door and spoke to Joe.

'Hi. Have you come to see Ellen? She's waiting for you.'

Then she gasped as she saw me.

'WHAT is that CAT doing in here?'

Joe turned and saw me. His mouth dropped open.

'I don't believe this. It's – it's our cat. He must have followed me.'

I gave Joe and the nurse a rebellious stare. I didn't even stop but kinked the end of my tail and went swanning through those wide doors on my own. I was going to see Ellen.

'You CHEEKY cat,' cried the nurse, and Joe started laughing. I heard the nurse calling out, 'Sister. Sister, we've got a cat in the ward.'

I kept walking, down the row of high beds, looking for Ellen. A well-timed meow did the trick. Ellen sat up on her bed with a squeal of surprise.

'SOLOMON!'

I must have leaped ten foot through the air from the floor to Ellen's bed. Then I was purring and purring and she was kissing me and crying and smiling all at once.

'How did you get here? You miracle cat,' she breathed. 'Oh it's so good to see you.'

We had a few precious minutes before Joe came down the ward with a contingent of fussing nurses.

'Livestock are strictly not permitted in this hospital,' said the one in the dark blue uniform. I'd never been described as livestock before, but I thought she must be the boss, so I gazed lovingly into her eyes as I cuddled up to Ellen.

'We will have to ask you to take him out immediately,' said the boss sister, but she had eye contact with me and I could see that she was admiring me. 'He's a lovely cat but …'

Joe was very persuasive. I saw a different side to him as he talked quietly to the nurses, telling them about me.

'He's beautifully clean, and he's good for Ellen. He'll make her better. Look, she's got more colour in her cheeks already.'

'Solomon is a healing cat,' said Ellen clearly from the bed. 'Please, please let him stay. Then Joe will take him home.'

The sister looked at Ellen in astonishment, then at Joe.

'That's the first time Ellen has spoken to us since she's been in the hospital,' she said. She stood, frowning for a moment then she made an announcement. 'I haven't seen this cat. You've got one hour.' She winked at Joe and walked briskly away, followed by the two nurses who were smiling.

'Thanks. You're a star,' said Joe.

'No,' said Ellen, 'Solomon is the star.'

CHAPTER EIGHT

THE MARMITE SANDWICH

Ellen came home after many weeks in hospital, but she wasn't better. She wasn't like the Ellen I knew and loved. Instead of a smile, she had a frown on her face. Her voice was loud and cross, and the sparkle had gone from her eyes. She snapped at John, and even at me. I was upset. I took to sitting in a corner, looking at her reproachfully and trying to find times when I could show her how much I loved her. When Joe was there, Ellen hardly spoke and when he was out she had frenzies of cleaning, or sometimes she just curled up on her bed and slept.

I asked my angel what was wrong.

'Ellen is homesick,' she said. 'And she misses her piano. Music is important for Ellen. It feeds her spirit.'

'So what can I do?' I asked.

'Just go on loving her,' said the angel. 'Her bigger problem is Joe. She has to find the courage to leave him.'

'Well, he's John's dad,' I said, remembering how proud I'd been of my kittens and how sad I'd been to say goodbye to them. At least I still had Jessica.

'But where will Ellen go?' I asked.

'It's Joe who has to go,' said the angel.

'And what will happen if Joe goes?'

'There will be peace.'

Peace. I sat for a while in the angel's veil of light, thinking of the times when Ellen had been peaceful. In the garden, playing the piano, playing with John or sitting with me on her lap. Times when Joe wasn't there.

'Pam will help you,' said the angel. 'She is a warrior.'

My angel was right. That afternoon, Pam came marching over to the caravan with a determined look on her face. She'd seen Ellen leaving to fetch John from school, and Pam was going to have a go at Joe.

She was wearing stripy mittens and a stripy hat that looked like a bumblebee. She took them off and sat down opposite Joe who was slouched in a corner, a can of beer in his hand.

I fancied playing with the bumblebee hat, but it wasn't quite the moment.

'You've got to stop this boozing,' Pam said.

'Why shouldn't I have a beer? I've only had one today.' Joe glowered at Pam. 'I enjoy it. Get that do you?'

Pam leaned forward and wagged her finger at Joe.

'Don't you get bolshy with me young man. I know what goes on. Eee – the place stinks like a brewery. What did I do when Ellen was ill, Joe?' Pam didn't wait for him to answer but got up and wagged her finger right in his face. 'I came in here and cleared up your cans and bottles. I did that for Ellen, not for you.'

I looked at Pam's aura and it had sparks that flashed as she ranted at Joe. Jessica chose that moment to come out of her cupboard. She sat next to Pam, washing and smirking at Joe, while I stayed on the windowsill doing my Buddha act.

'I'm not afraid of you.' Pam's eyes burned at Joe but he wouldn't look at her.

'Give it a rest, Pam,' he growled, but Pam would not be stopped.

'Poor Ellen. That's what I say. OK, times are tough but you should pull together – not boozing and lying about the place while Ellen can hardly put food on the table. And look at John. When did you last buy him a decent set of clothes? He hasn't even got a P.E. kit for school. Oh he's cried to me about it, and I'm always giving him sandwiches, he's always hungry. And these cats. They know where to come for a meal. And do you ever say thank you? Do you? Go on, answer me.'

Jessica was really enjoying this. Her eyes were glitzy and she was washing her pink paws flamboyantly. She was taunting Joe.

He hung his head and stared at the floor, and in the end I felt sorry for him. Very carefully, I crept onto his lap.

'No purring,' said my angel.

Joe gave a huge sigh as if he was a balloon. He began

to stroke me with his rough hand and I knew my friend-liness was helping him.

'The truth is, Pam– ' he said at last. 'I know, I do drink too much. I feel so useless. I'm unemployed, and yeah I do lose my temper sometimes.'

'Now you're talking.' Pam sat back, looking satisfied. The sparks in her aura subsided and Jessica did some-thing I'd never seen her do before. She climbed up and wrapped herself around Pam's neck like a scarf, peeping round at her cheekily.

'You daft cat.'

Joe went on telling his hard luck story to Pam, and my angel said, 'Everyone's getting too serious.' It was time to play.

On the floor was an empty plastic carrier bag. I crouched and dived inside it head first, making it skid across the floor. I must have looked ridiculous with my tail and back legs sticking out. Then I rolled over and over inside the bag making it rustle. I sat in there like a flat cat and stared out, planning the next pounce. I made myself look wild, with goggling eyes and a loopy loopy tail. I charged out of the bag, skidded down to the bedroom, bounced off the door and dived back into the plastic bag. Joe and Pam were laughing louder and louder as I thought of more tricks to perform.

'Eee,' said Pam, rubbing her eyes. 'That's what we need, a good laugh. That cat knows exactly what he's doing, don't you Solomon?'

By the time Ellen came back we were happy, and Joe had picked up his beer cans and started making tea.

John burst into the caravan, his face bright and alive.

'Look at my book. I got a gold star.'

'A gold star! Eee,' said Pam. 'Good boy.'

'Look Solomon,' John thrust his school book in front of my face, 'that's you.'

I stared in surprise. John had done a picture of me with my tail up and a big smile on my face. He'd coloured me black with yellow paws and a yellow nose, and he'd done my whiskers in rainbow colours. He'd drawn a big heart next to me, coloured it red, and written, 'I love Solomon. He's the best cat.'

I touched noses with the picture of me, and everyone laughed. Pam pointed at a splodge John had drawn in the air above my head. He'd coloured it pink and gold with tiny stars and a smiley face.

'Who's that?' Pam asked.

'That's Solomon's angel,' John said, and everyone looked at each other as if John had said something amazing.

Joe did try to be good after the telling off he'd had from Pam. All of us tried, even Jessica, but I guess we knew it couldn't last, and it didn't. The last truly happy day was the day it snowed.

Jessica and I went out and played penguins. It was our

favourite game now. We'd seen penguins on television, and sat mesmerised, watching them sliding over the ice. Jessica had gone up to the screen and patted one with her paws and tried to catch it, growling with annoyance when she found it wasn't possible. We'd had a go at playing penguins in our old home, skidding across the kitchen floor on our tummies. Jessica would lie on her side and slide round the edge of the rug kicking it with her back feet as if she was riding a bike.

So when we saw the sheen of new snow in the morning sun, we looked at each other. Penguins! Out in the snow we went mad, racing and sliding down the slippery path until our paws burned with the cold, and everyone was laughing at us. Later we sat in the caravan window and watched John, Ellen and Joe building an enormous snowman.

I was OK with it, but the snowman really spooked Jessica. Joe put a baseball cap on its head and lifted John up to put in two black eyes and a carrot nose. The snowman looked alive. Jessica's neck got longer and longer. She vanished into her cupboard and stayed there.

The snow melted quickly, but the snowman's head hung around for days looking at everyone who passed, especially Jessica.

We were glad when spring came and the sun warmed everything. Jessica and I played outside in the spring evenings, and in the twilight we hid in the copse and watched the baby badgers squealing and playing.

'They remind me of our kittens,' Jessica said sadly. 'I wish we could have some more.'

'We can't,' I said. 'Ellen explained all that to us after we'd been to the vet. She said there were already too many unwanted kittens in the world, and feral cats that don't have homes.'

Spring turned to summer, and we might have all been happy if it hadn't been for Joe's behaviour. It came to a head one terrible day that was to change our lives.

It was late summer and John had gone back to school after his long summer holiday.

I knew that something was going to happen when Joe got up early, shaved his face and put on his black leather jacket. Ellen tipped the money out of her purse and sat at the table counting it. She gave some to Joe.

'That's for petrol.'

He didn't say thank you but looked at the money angrily. 'That won't get me far.'

'It's enough. I need the rest for our food,' said Ellen.

'How am I supposed to get lunch with that?'

'I made you a sandwich.'

'What's in it?'

'Marmite. It's all we've got.'

'I don't want a Marmite sandwich,' Joe roared suddenly, and he snatched the tinfoil package from Ellen and threw it, splat, on the floor.

Ellen looked furious.

'You ungrateful PIG,' she yelled. 'I've given you money, I've ironed your shirt and I've made you a sand-wich. Now you chuck it on the floor.'

I knew what was going to happen next, and it did.

Jessica grabbed the Marmite sandwich between her teeth and reversed out of the cat flap with it.

'Serves you right,' said Ellen.'I'm not making another one.'

Joe wrenched the door open, his eyes glittering with rage.

'Don't call ME a pig! I happen to like a pint and a pasty for my lunch, if you weren't too mean to give me the money.'

'What you mean is *six* pints and a pasty,' said Ellen. 'I thought you were going to look for work, Joe? You keep off the drink when you're driving.'

'Yeah, yeah. Stop nagging me, woman.'

Joe looked at Ellen as if he hated her. A glow of strength came into Ellen's eyes. I felt like cheering. The real Ellen was back, good and bright and very stubborn. She marched to the caravan door and stood there like a warrior, her golden hair rippling in the wind. Beside her was the tallest of angels, its brilliance sparking across the grass and lighting up the moisture that hung from the trees, turning the raindrops into fairy lights. The angel brandished a sword of light and stuck it into the earth between Joe and Ellen. I could see the jewelled handle sparkling and I heard the angel cry out, 'It is done.'

Ellen looked ready to explode with the words she wanted to scream at Joe. But the angel had wrapped a shimmering cloak around her, and she stayed silent. She turned her back on Joe, swept into the caravan and shut the door.

'Sanctimonious cow,' he yelled and flung himself into the car, fired the engine and left in a screech of tyres. Meanwhile, Jessica stayed under the caravan picking the tinfoil off the Marmite sandwich in little strips of silver.

I followed Ellen into John's bedroom, and his teddy bears had a conspiratorial twinkle in their eyes as if they shared some secret knowledge. Ellen sat down on John's bed with me on her lap. She didn't say a word but just rocked me and stroked my tingling fur, her hands moving from my head to the tip of my tail.

We stared out of the window at a hard shower of rain which passed over, leaving a dark cloud with a beautiful rainbow. Ellen seemed to stop breathing as she gazed at it, and then she began to tell me a story.

'They say that a rainbow is a promise, Solomon,' she said in her bewitching storytelling voice. 'And there's a legend that the rainbow is really a bridge, and when dogs and cats die they go over the rainbow bridge into a beautiful land where they wait for their loved ones to join them. When you die you'll wait for me, won't you Solomon?'

I purred and stretched my paws out, one on each side of her neck as if I was hugging her. Today she needed me to be extra loving. But when Ellen told me why, I didn't believe her. I thought it was part of the story.

'I'm going away, Solomon, with John, and I can't take you …' She started to cry. 'I can't take you. No one will let me have a cat, and I have to leave Joe, Solomon, I have to. Do you understand?'

I did, but I didn't believe her.

'I want you to stay here, Solomon, and wait for me, like the cats by the rainbow bridge. You and Jessica must stay here. And when I've found a place, I'll come back for you and … and we'll be together again. I promise.'

I purred and snuggled into her neck, but still I didn't believe her.

Everyone except me seemed to know what was going to happen that day. My angel tried to talk to me but I wouldn't listen. It was something I didn't want to face.

Suddenly Ellen put me down. She rummaged in her handbag and fished out a plastic card with numbers and letters on it. She stared at it for long minutes. She turned on some loud music and pranced around, picking things up and piling them on the table. She opened a cupboard and dragged out a big bag, unzipped it and put the stuff inside.

Ellen put some of John's toys into another bag. His

shoes and wellies, his pyjamas and two teddies were stuffed in and zipped up. Ellen lugged the two bags outside and hid them under the caravan. She spread a map out on the table and studied it, talking on the phone with the plastic card in her other hand. She kept looking at me, and several times I heard her asking 'Do you take cats?' and the funny little voice inside the phone was saying, 'No.'

Joe came back in an ugly temper. He chucked the car keys on the table and headed for the fridge.

'Don't ask,' he growled at Ellen. 'Just let me have a drink.'

He didn't kiss her or ask how she was. He didn't even look at her.

'I'm going to fetch John.' Ellen took the keys and I followed her outside. She picked me up, and I could feel her heart beating very fast and she was trembling.

'You go and hide, Solomon,' she whispered to me. 'Go and be with Jessica. And whatever happens, I promise I'll come back for you. You must stay here, Solomon. Promise you will stay.'

I stared at her, and she started to cry and put me down on the grass. Moving furtively, she slid the two bags out and loaded them into the car.

'Where do you think you're going?' Joe towered in the doorway.

Ellen stood very straight and looked back at him.

'I'm leaving you, Joe,' she said firmly. 'And I'm taking John. And I'm NEVER coming back.'

She had the car engine running and she jumped in and drove away.

Joe roared and raged. He ran after the car, hurling beer cans at it. I escaped into the hedge and watched, terrified, as he stomped back into the caravan, swearing. There were bangs and crashes as he hurled things around, breaking china and kicking doors. The whole caravan was shuddering. I felt I could never go in there, ever again.

Ellen had gone. She had left me behind.

I was devastated.

But Jessica was still under the caravan unwrapping the Marmite sandwich.

CHAPTER NINE

ABANDONED

I felt betrayed. I'd done my best, my very best, and now I'd been abandoned. I'd been loyal, and kind, I'd set off alone as a tiny kitten to find Ellen, and then I'd been brave and visited her in hospital. And look what happened. She abandoned me.

I was deeply upset, but I couldn't sit around crying like a human. It seemed easier to be angry.

My angel tried to intervene.

'It will get worse,' she said. 'But you must try to survive and wait for Ellen.'

I didn't want to listen. Flicking my tail in annoyance, I turned my back on the shining angel and went to find Jessica. She would teach me how to be angry, and how to survive in the wild.

We sat up for most of the night on the mossy branch watching the caravan. Joe ranted and thundered around for hours. He kept flinging the door open and chucking things out into the night. Between showers the moon was bright and we could see Ellen's stuff lying in the wet grass: her clothes, her books, her pot plants, her CDs.

Nick came plodding down the path with Paisley on a lead. Paisley didn't want to go near the caravan, and Nick had to drag him.

'You useless great mutt. Daft as a brush you are.' In the end Nick tied Paisley to a lamppost. 'Stay there.'

He hammered on the door and Joe wrenched it open. In the lamplight his eyes were red, and he had a bottle in his hand.

'What's going on?' Nick asked. 'I've had complaints. And what's all the stuff doing out here?'

'She's left me. That's what's wrong. And she's taken MY son.'

'Well I don't blame her if you carry on like that,' said Nick. Joe started ranting and swearing. He sat down on the caravan steps.

'Now you quieten down,' Nick said calmly. 'It's no good carrying on like this, Joe. I'm sorry for you, but this is my campsite and if you don't calm down and pick up this mess, then we'll be having a serious talk in the morning about whether I can let you stay here.'

Joe put his head in his hands and sobbed like a child, sobs that shook his big body. Normally I would have run to him and calmed him down with my powerful purr. But I was an angry cat now.

'Come on, inside. You've had a skinful.' Nick spoke kindly to Joe, steered him into the caravan and shut the door. Paisley was whining and winding his lead round and round the lamppost until he'd nearly strangled himself.

The door opened again and Nick came out.

'You sleep it off, Joe. We'll sort it out in the morning,' he said, and turned off the caravan lights. He unwrapped Paisley from the lamppost and plodded off into the dark, tutting and grumbling.

Jessica was cold, so we headed for the badger hole and curled up together, trying to sleep. Our fur was wet, and we were hungry, but at least we had a safe place out of the rain. My angel tried to talk to me again, but I refused to listen. I blocked my mind and sank into a deep sleep.

In my sleep I dreamed a beautiful dream. I dreamed of the previous life I had had with Ellen, when she was a child, and I was her cat.

When Ellen was a child she wouldn't speak. She knew how to talk but chose not to, and that got her into lots of trouble. People thought she was being sullen, or snobby, or even rude, and Ellen was none of those things. She was telepathic, and that's why I was the perfect cat for her – we could read each other's silent thoughts.

In that lifetime I was devoted to Ellen. I followed her down the road to school, and in the afternoons I ran to meet her when she returned, her face pale and her eyes full of pain. As soon as she saw me Ellen came alive again and we danced in the garden, or she let me sit on the piano while she played the black and white keys with her small hands. I loved music and the vibrations of it tingled in my fur. Sometimes Ellen played sad music and I'd lie with my chin on the piano top, watching her eyes and sharing those deep feelings with her. Then she'd play fast melodies that rippled through the house and through my bones.

I heard the same music now, in my dream, and I was a dancing cat, whirling on the lawn with Ellen who loved to dance so much. The air was alive with coloured ribbons and we were generating happiness. It was billowing out from the garden in clouds of stars, all fizzing and popping, and crowds of people were gathering round us in a circle. They had come for healing, bringing their sad faces and their troubles, and Ellen and I were a wild child and a wild cat turning sadness into joy.

Ellen's face shone in my dream, she was looking at me, holding me and saying, 'Wait for me, Solomon. Wait and I will come back for you.'

The music in my dream changed and I awoke to the sound of pouring rain, the whole copse dripping with silvery drops and water that gurgled down the lane.

When the rain was over Jessica gave me a demonstration of how to hunt mice. Catching them was no problem for me, but finding them in a copse full of soaking wet leaves was difficult. Jessica knew exactly where they were and she quietly caught two and gave one to me.

'It's no good just practising pounces,' she said. 'You've got to watch and smell out the places where they live.'

'I'd rather have Whiskas rabbit,' I said.

'Poof,' she said. 'Tinned stuff? This is the real deal.'

Later that morning we went to look at the caravan. Joe's bedroom curtains were still drawn and it was quiet. Pam was outside talking to Nick, and they were picking up the dripping wet things Joe had thrown out, putting them all into a black bag. I wanted to run to Pam. She would give me a cuddle and a compliment, and probably a meal.

'No,' said Jessica. 'Look what's happening now. They've got the cat basket.'

Pam was dragging our travelling basket out from under the caravan.

'I can catch them, easy,' she said. 'They know me.'

'You hang on to the basket then, Pam,' said Nick. 'It's a bit premature to catch the cats yet. Wait till Joe's sober and he might want them. But he'll have to go. I can't be doing with this.'

'Ellen worshipped those cats,' said Pam. 'But if she's not coming back and she can't find a place to rent that takes cats, they've got to go somewhere. The RSPCA will find homes for them.'

I knew that word. RSPCA. Pam stood there swinging the cat basket, and I remembered how firmly Joe had stuffed us both in there. Jessica and I looked at each other. We didn't need to say it. We would have to disappear, go deep into the countryside and live like wild cats.

I watched Pam for one more minute. She'd been a good friend, and I would have liked to say goodbye. I saw her walk across to something else that Joe had thrown out of the caravan. She picked it up slowly.

'Eee. Ellen loved this. What a shame.' She held up the amber velvet cushion. It was sopping wet and the drops glistened on the beautiful velvet.

'I'll look after this,' Pam said to Nick. 'I'm going to wash it, dry it out and make it nice again.'

She walked away with the cat basket in one hand and the amber velvet cushion in the other. I so wanted to run after Pam. If only I'd known what was going to happen, I would have jumped into that cat basket and dragged Jessica in with me.

Jessica was already trotting purposefully through the copse however. Her instinct was strong. She wouldn't hang around. I followed her dubiously over the far hedge and across the fields, on and on she led me, and she wouldn't turn around. She paused only once, to hiss at a cow who had lowered her head to sniff at her. At the far end of the field we crossed a stone stile into the deep woods. My angel tried to speak to me, and I ignored her. She was trying to tell me to let Jessica go, but I wouldn't. Jessica needed me, and I needed her.

The stone stile seemed like a bridge to another world: green pathways, and mossy banks and ferns. Ancient trees with roots curling into stone walls, hollows, and holes full of leaves. I was aware of tiny faces watching us, other creatures who lived in the wood, fairy folk and gnomes. Jessica had obviously been in the enchanted wood before. She led me to a dry cave under a beech tree. It was lined with springy moss and a deep bed of rustling beech leaves.

Our place. It was OK. Even better than the badger hole, which was too close to the caravan. We didn't want to be found and put in that cat cage.

That first night, I couldn't sleep. Jessica curled up and tucked her tail neatly around her pink paws. Looking at her sleeping face I felt the need to be on guard like a dog. I listened to the noises of the wood, the wind whistling in the treetops, the familiar shuffling of badgers, the brisk trot of a passing fox, and the smaller scrabblings of mice and birds. There were no human sounds at all.

I'd never been a wild cat in any of my lifetimes. It spooked me. I'd always had a human to turn to. I'd never before had no owner to love. Now I had gone twenty-four hours without purring. I ached inside. I wanted Ellen and John. But I didn't tell Jessica.

Gradually we became used to being cold and wet

most of the time and hunting for our food. We developed a routine of eating, washing and sleeping. In the early days we had some fun times too, chasing each other and climbing trees. Jessica seemed different from the way she had been with humans.

'What about your dream of going to live with an old lady?' I asked her.

'Oh that can wait,' she said. 'Right now I'm having fun.'

'I'm not,' I said. 'It's not what I want to do with my life.'

'But this is a holiday,' said Jessica. 'Can't you enjoy it?'

I thought about it.

'No,' I said. 'I feel angry, and abandoned.'

'You've got me.' Jessica gave me a sweet little kiss on the nose and I felt better.

The morning was still and sunny. We wanted to be out of the shady wood with the warmth of the winter sun on our fur. Instead of going back towards the caravan site, Jessica chose to head out of the other side of the wood. We trotted along a tarmac lane and over a high bridge spanning a busy road.

Seeing the road disturbed me. We crouched down and peeked through the railings at the lorries and cars roaring and swooshing along below us. My psi sense was suddenly activated and I turned to face north and stare at the long road curving into the distance. The road home. The road back to the beautiful house where we had lived with Ellen. I stood up and stuck my head through the railings, wondering if it would be possible to jump down onto the roof of a speeding lorry.

'Don't do it,' said Jessica, and she led me firmly away from the bridge. She turned and looked at me cheekily, sparking her golden eyes in the way she always did when she had a secret.

She ran on up the lane and round the edge of a stubble field. The light was changing to an electric brilliance, and there was a new sound in the air, a sound I'd never heard before. Where was Jessica taking me?

We ran up a hill covered in tufty wiry grass, and the horizon was so bright now it was like running up to the sky. I followed Jessica right to the shining edge of it. We sat down and gazed in astonishment at the expanse of glittering turquoise water. It stretched far away to where the horizon was a dark blue line, and all of it was singing and swishing with waves.

'What is it?' I asked Jessica.

'It's the sea.'

I was awestruck. Now I understood why John had always jumped around and screamed with excitement when Ellen said they were going to the sea. Seeing such a feast of dazzling light and space was incredible.

'How did you know about it?' I asked.

'In my last lifetime I was a ship's cat,' said Jessica, 'and

I loved it. The ship was like a big floating house and I was the only cat. But once, I fell in and a brave sailor jumped over the side and rescued me. I was freezing cold and my fur tasted salty. After that they spoilt me and I got fat and lazy.'

'So why did you bring me here today?'

Jessica looked thoughtful. 'Every cat should see the sea just once before they die,' she said. 'You need to know what wonderful things are out there.'

I looked at Jessica with new respect. She had brought me here as a treat, to distract me from my sorrow at losing Ellen.

We stayed on the cliff top, dozing with the sun on our faces, and I kept opening my eyes a crack and soaking up the energy of the sparkles that danced on the water.

Jessica was hungry, and she knew exactly where to go. She led me along the cliff path, winding between gorse and heather and rocks, a long way down to a cove with a harbour and boats. People were strolling about in the sunshine but she avoided them and ran along the harbour wall. I followed, nervously. The water was deep and so far below the wall, with splashing waves on one side and translucent green on the other. It looked cold. The stone quay smelled of fish and there were piles of rope and lobster pots lying around.

It made me hungry, but as much as I was enjoying all

the new sights and sounds, I didn't want to be there. I wanted to be at home, in Ellen's arms, and the moment of missing her was so painful that I lost my awareness of what Jessica intended to do. My angel tried to warn me to stop her, but it was too late.

One minute Jessica was there with me as we crouched on the edge of the wall looking down at a gently rocking boat. She turned and gave me that cheeky 'I dare you' look. Her golden eyes danced teasingly into mine. The next minute she did a breathtaking jump. I saw her fly downwards with her white-tipped paws wide apart, her tail snaking. She landed on the deck of the boat and found herself a perch on top of a coil of blue rope. Her bright face looked up at me expectantly.

I was distraught. I couldn't possibly jump down there. Or could I? While I was weaving to and fro and thinking about it, something dreadful happened. The boat's engine throbbed into life and it started to pull away from the wall. I wailed in panic. I was losing Jessica! Shocked, I watched the boat turn in a curve of white water and head out of the harbour. I could see the man in the glass cabin, driving it, not knowing he had a cat on board. I watched Jessica getting smaller and smaller until she was no bigger than an ant – she was only a black speck and I couldn't see her buttercup eyes or hear her meows any more.

How had I let this happen? I had lost Jessica. She

might never come back. She had found herself another life as a ship's cat, and I was again abandoned, left alone on a harbour wall with a pain in my tummy from hunger, and a new pain in my fast beating heart. I was like an empty cat. Not a purring happy cat. A shell of a cat with nothing to eat, nowhere to go, no one to love.

I glanced at the people walking along the quay. They had warm coats. I longed to be in someone's arms, purring into one of those squashy coats, finding a heartbeat. Attaching myself to a new human would be easy for me. But I couldn't leave Jessica. I had to stay there and watch the distant boat tossing on the waves. It was so far away now, I wasn't sure if I was looking at the right boat, there were so many out there. So I sat steadfastly on the edge of the quay. The stones were warm from the sun but a chilly breeze was blowing. It was late afternoon and we should have been heading back to our cave in the beech wood.

I'd been with Jessica for three years now. We'd shared so much. We still played together and slept blissfully curled into each other. Forever friends. Or so I'd thought.

The afternoon sun was low and the water blazed pink. Then I heard a sound that gave me a jolt. A little boy's voice.

'Look, Mummy. A cat!'

He sounded so like John that I turned and automatically put my tail up, only to see it wasn't John and it wasn't Ellen. But it was a family, and they obviously liked cats.

'Don't go with them,' said my angel.

But I purred and kinked my back and rubbed against their legs. It was second nature to me. Four of them were stroking me – a mum, dad and two young boys who were kind and loving.

'He looks like a stray,' the mum said. 'He's so thin, and his fur feels rough.' She looked into my eyes. 'Are you all right, pussy cat?'

No, I wasn't all right. I was alone and broken hearted. But I still knew how to purr.

'Would you like to come home with us?' she asked.

'Oh please Mummy, let's take him.'

'Please. He's lovely. He'll get cold out here.'

'You can't do that,' said the dad. 'He might be some-one's cat. Tell you what – we'll come back tomorrow and if he's still hanging around, he must be a stray and we'll take him home.'

'Don't go with them,' said my angel again.

I had a decision to make.

'But I've lost everything,' I said to my angel.

'No you haven't, Solomon. You've got me,' she said.

'But you haven't got fur,' I said. Sadness filled me as I walked away from the family and slumped down beside a pile of smelly lobster pots. The woman came after me and picked me up. I leaned on her red fleece jacket and listened to her heartbeat for a few precious minutes, and it seemed to recharge me for what I had to do.

She put me down.

'He's got fleas.' She brushed at her coat, and I flicked my tail, embarrassed. I'd never had fleas before. Ellen had seen to that. Now they were all over me, driving me crazy sometimes so that I tore and scratched at my fur. I'd been proud of my glossy coat. Sadly, I turned my back on that nice family and sat watching the sea.

'I expect he's a fisherman's cat,' I heard her say.

I was too upset to watch them walking away. I imagined their home with a cosy fire burning. As evening settled over the sea, I got colder and colder. I huddled against a pile of wet rope and netting, trying to shelter from the wind. Tonight I wouldn't have Jessica to keep me warm. Would she miss me too? I focused on a bright star that was shining in the evening sky, and pretended it was Jessica.

The night dragged on and on. My loneliness deepened with the darkness, and so did the hunger. To keep warm I tucked my paws under my body and eventually fell asleep. No one came. No one walked by and noticed me. The seagulls were the only living creatures in that cold, cold place and I awoke to see them sitting motionless along the wall, their yellow eyes glinting in the dawn.

The sea and the sky flushed crimson, and one by one

the boats returned to the harbour. I watched for Jessica, but she didn't come. I considered making the long trek back to our cave in the beech wood, if I could find the way. I thought about living there alone. Or trying to find Ellen.

Or just surviving.

Or willing myself to die.

Miserably I stared at the last boat coming in, and as it turned towards the harbour the rising sun flashed on the windows of the cabin. And there, silhouetted against the brightness, was the bulk of a fisherman and a tiny cat, a black cat who was in the cabin with him, her paws up on the window, her face gazing towards the harbour. The boat came in closer and the cat's face was black and white with a little pink nose, and eyes that shone as yellow as the sun. My Jessica!

I puffed my chest out and arched my whiskers. I knew Jessica could see me there waiting. And I knew she loved me. She was staring at me, and my heart was full of joy.

I followed along the quay as the boat chugged towards a flight of dark green stone steps. The fisherman carried Jessica out of the cabin and put her on the steps. She looked back at him and meowed, and stood there with her tail up. What was she waiting for? Hadn't she seen me?

The fisherman lifted the lid of a huge black basket,

and instantly the seagulls screamed and twirled around the boat in a flurry of white wings. He took out a fish and gave it to Jessica. She started up the steps with it in her mouth, and the seagulls were dive bombing her. But Jessica hung on to her fish, glaring and growling at the fierce birds. I was afraid for her. More and more gulls were coming from far and wide, squabbling and screeching.

'Get off!' The fisherman came to her rescue by chucking some more fish into the water, diverting the birds away from Jessica. She kept coming up the steps with the heavy fish, and I was so proud of her I thought I would burst with gratitude.

She'd come back, and she'd brought us a meal fit for a king.

Amidst my joy, what happened next was unthinkable.

I had no reason to be afraid of a human. No human had ever hurt me. So I didn't turn around when heavy footsteps came up behind me. Two big hands picked me up and I was so surprised I didn't resist at all.

'I've got him,' the man said and took me over to where a woman in a red fleece jacket was standing next to a plastic cage. I looked back at Jessica who was nearly at the top of the steps, the fish still in her mouth, and she hesitated when she saw me being carried away.

'In you go.' The man pushed me into the cat cage and shut the hatch. I turned around, meowing desperately at Jessica.

'Lucky he was still here,' said the woman. 'He's definitely a stray.'

She put her face up to the cage and looked in at me. 'Don't you worry pussy cat. We'll give you a nice home, and get rid of those fleas for you. You shall have a warm bed and plenty to eat.'

I meowed very loudly, my voice echoing all over the harbour as the man put the cat cage in the back of a van. I could see Jessica sitting under a bench with her fish, out of reach of the seagulls. She was watching me, with anxious eyes. I should have been there, kissing her, welcoming her back after our time apart. That sweet moment of reunion had been snatched away.

I knew now that I didn't want a new home. I wanted to stay with Jessica and survive in the wild until Ellen came back for us.

How had I got it so wrong?

My last glimpse was of Jessica's disappointed face, and then the doors of the van clicked shut. The couple got in and started the engine, talking happily.

'Well, fancy us finding a lovely cat when we're on holiday. The boys are gonna love him. I wonder what his name is.'

'How about Blackie? Or Socks? Or Fred? That's it. Fred. We'll call him Fred.'

Fred! I was to be called Fred. It sounded so final. It felt like the end of everything for me. I was a failure.

Not only had I let Jessica down when she'd been so brave, but I'd disobeyed my angel. I'd been too trusting.

Another terrible thought surfaced. What if these well-meaning people took me far away to another place? What if I never saw Jessica again? Fight, I thought. Come on Solomon – fight!

I'd always been a quiet, peaceful cat. But now, as the van drove away, I did something I'd never done before. I panicked.

My claws came out. My lips curled back. My tail lashed and banged the sides of the cage. I ripped and tore at the plastic, I pinged the metal grille that was keeping me prisoner. I shredded the cushion and savaged the white stuffing inside. Fight, I kept thinking, fight. Once I'd started I couldn't stop.

'He's going berserk,' said the woman. 'Stop the car, Bill. He's going crazy.'

'Nah, he'll be all right. He'll have to settle down if we're going all the way to London, won't he?'

I yowled and screamed. I gnawed at the plastic round the edge of the metal grille I was in such a frenzy that my fur was coming out, and then, to my shame, I peed into the cushion and the cage stank of it. My teeth and my nose started to bleed and sting, the pads of my paws burned, and my heart was going at white-hot speed.

'Bill, you MUST STOP. We can't let him get in such a state, he'll hurt himself.' The woman reached over and slid the cage round to look at me. 'He's killing himself. He's covered in blood. Will you stop, PLEASE? Let me see if I can calm him down.'

'I can't stop on this busy road.'

'Turn off into one of the side streets.'

'OK, OK.'

I was getting hotter and hotter and my pulse was roaring in my ears. The van stopped, and they both got out and opened the back doors. The fresh salty air came blowing in. It calmed me just a little. The woman was talking to me but I didn't listen. I went on yowling and scrabbling.

'Look at the state of him. I've got to get him out. I'll wrap him in my coat and have him on my lap.'

'You can't do that. He'll run wild in the car and cause an accident.'

I searched the woman's eyes, willing her to understand, and she did.

'It's obvious he doesn't want to come with us. I don't care what you think, I'm letting him out.'

'Don't let him go. We should take him back to the harbour. Have some sense. You can't let him go in the street.'

The woman was determined. She had seen my desperation. She undid the catch and lifted the grille. She reached in to pick me up but I sprang out like a tiger and belted down the strange road, my tail kinked, my paws on fire. Instinctively I ran into the wind towards the shining sea. I dashed across roads, and cars squealed their brakes as they tried to avoid me. I ran down a cobbled street, past shops and in and out of people. I stopped on a beautiful square of grass where there was a stone obelisk with wreaths of red poppies stacked around it. No one was there so I sat on the stone steps and tried to stop trembling. I was free now. I could hear the seagulls and see the water sparkling in the distance. But I was totally lost. I licked the blood from my white-tipped paws, and lapped cool water from a puddle at the foot of the steps.

I hurt all over, but finding Jessica was my priority.

Getting into a frenzy had been traumatic for a cat like me, and I needed time to recover. The amber velvet cushion was what I longed for, and Ellen's loving hands stroking me. The stillness and peace of that patch of grass was all I had to calm myself down while I figured out how to get back to the harbour.

I was in a town, high on a hill, and between the houses were views of the shining sea. My eyes were drawn to the sheet of sunlight on water, and a memory floated into my mind. 'My light is so bright that I become almost invisible on earth, but if you look at sparkles you will see me, especially in the sunlight glinting on water.' The Angel of the Silver Stars had whispered those words into my soul before I was born. I sat still and focused on the shining water, and I felt a change. It drifted around me like snowflakes, each one full of clustered stars. My angel was covering me in healing sparks. She wasn't telling me off for ignoring her. She was loving me.

'Take time to rest in this special place, Solomon,' she said. 'Rest and sleep, and when the sun goes down, the bright star will guide you back to Jessica.'

I curled up on the soft grass at the edge of the steps. It was springy, like a cushion, and the warm smell of the earth helped me to relax. People and cars were passing by but no one took any notice of a black cat curled up asleep. My sleep was deep and healing, and when I woke up and stretched, the sun had gone down, the sky was orange and duck-egg green, and in the green part was Jessica's bright star, just rising.

My paws were sore. But now I was free and full of hope. I headed downhill towards the sea, and the cobbled streets were cool under my pads. Down and down I trotted, following the bright star, until the view of the harbour opened up before me. The evening sea was pink and silver. Seagulls sat motionless along the railings. Where was Jessica?

I listened.

I heard the waves, and the wind, and the seagulls. I heard music and voices in the town behind me.

'Keep listening,' said my angel.

And then I heard Jessica. Her particular high-pitched

meow, again and again. She was calling me. I meowed back and she came running. We kissed and purred and rubbed against each other. Feeling her silky warm coat was a coming home for me.

I'd expected Jessica to tell me off, or even give me a swipe for being so stupid, but she was kind and welcoming. I felt very lucky. She licked my face for me and sniffed at my sore paws. They were bruised and swollen from my panic and the long run through the streets, and now I could hardly walk on them.

Jessica led me to the nest she had made in a pile of netting and rope. We snuggled together, looking out at the darkening sea.

'That's your star,' I said. 'When you'd gone on the boat I stared at it and imagined it was you. Then my angel told me to follow it, and it led me back here from miles up the hill.'

Jessica looked pensive.

'I wish I had an angel like you've got,' she said.

I was horrified.

'Of course you have one,' I said. 'Every cat has.'

'But I've never seen mine,' she said.

'I'll teach you how to. When the sun rises again.'

'Won't the moon do? Look!'

We peered out and saw a white moon and a path of silver glistening on the water.

'Let's never be apart again,' I said as we sat pressed

close together in the moonlight.

'No,' she agreed. 'Let's vow never to leave each other.'

'Together forever,' I said, and we touched noses.

Later I was to look back with gratitude and realise that this trip to the sea was Jessica's last amazing gift to me.

CHAPTER TEN

THE DIARY OF A DESPERATE CAT

We stayed at the harbour for a few wonderful days, allowing my paws to heal. The rest and the meals of fresh fish did us good. Every morning Jessica ran down the steps with her tail up to meet the fisherman she had made friends with, and he gave her a fish that was like the biggest sardine in the world. Its skin shone with green and purple, and it tasted delicious to us. Jessica managed to share it with me without growling, so I felt very special and loved.

We even talked of setting up home in this sunny harbour. Until one morning there was no light on the water, and the stone quay was trembling with the pounding of waves. The seagulls stood hunched with their beaks to the wind, and when they were flying, the gale was blowing them backwards. Jessica and I were curled together, keeping each other warm, and we didn't want to put our heads out into the storm. But the waves got louder and more powerful as the tide surged in. Hard white beads of spray splattered across the quay, and cold salty water came sweeping right under our nest.

'Move … quickly!' said Jessica 'Or we'll be washed into the sea.'

Horrified, we looked outside and saw clouds of spray exploding high into the air, hissing across the quay like hail. A swerving mass of white moved between us and the safety of the land.

'RUN!'

My paws were still tender, but I dashed after Jessica, following her flying figure along the quay with the wind whisking us through the spray, perilously close to the edge.

'Don't let us die in that wild sea,' I prayed as I ran, my paws skidding on bits of seaweed, and my fur drenched by the flying spray. I don't know how we got to the cliff path but we did, and there we were sheltered from the wind by banks of heather and thrift. The path was like a low tunnel with the wind whistling overhead.

We both knew our holiday was over. There would be no more fish and no more gazing at a sunlit sea. Winter storms were chasing us inland, back to the safety of our cave under the beech tree. We didn't stop to talk. After the first mad dash we slowed to a steady trot and all I had to do was follow Jessica. Over the fields and into the woods where the wind in the high branches roared like the wild sea.

Our fur was wet and we looked spikey and bedraggled when we finally arrived at the beech cave. It was comforting to find that more dry leaves had been blown in and piled up inside. We settled in with much rustling, and licked each other's wet fur. I remembered how kindly Ellen used to dry me with a soft towel if I'd been out in the rain. I remembered the radiator, the sofa and the amber velvet cushion.

Where was Ellen now, and what would she think if she saw us soaking wet, shivering and hungry? Facing a winter in the wild wood, living on mice, surviving cold nights with only each other and a pile of beech leaves to keep us warm.

As the last leaves fell from the trees, the days got shorter and darker, the nights longer, and the home-sickness deeper. Without Jessica I couldn't have endured it. She was an expert hunter, better than me, and even when the mice had disappeared for the winter, she still managed to find one, and sometimes, one each. But I still thought longingly of the easy, tasty cat food Ellen used to give us.

Through the long nights I stayed awake, thinking of the piano and how I'd loved to sit on it while Ellen played. I thought about little John showing me his picture of me, and Pam calling me a 'heaven sent cat'. I even thought of Joe and how warm he was to sit on, and how he'd cried when I gave him healing. Where were they all now?

After we had lived wild for several weeks, I was awoken one night by a terrible yowling and screaming sound nearby. Jessica was not in the cave with me, although this wasn't unusual as sometimes she went out early to hunt for mice while it was still dark.

I crept out of the cave and sat listening. Above me the stars were tangled in the bare branches of the wood, and the twiggy silhouettes of rooks' nests. It was silent. Then the yowling and screaming began again, and the crashing sound of two animals rolling and struggling with each other.

I saw Jessica come running back, low to the ground, her black and white face clearly visible through the dark trees. She crawled into our cave and collapsed. She'd had a fight with a feral cat and it had bitten her on the neck. She was shaking violently and breathing very fast.

Concerned, I sniffed at the wound on her neck, but she wouldn't let me touch it. All day she lay there, exhausted, and I went out to catch mice on my own. I brought her one but she wouldn't eat. She just wanted to sleep.

I inspected her fur and found she was in poor condition. She was thin, and her coat was dull. Along her back she had patches of bare skin. Mine was the same. We were both suffering from living wild in the cold damp winter. Some days the weather was so bad we'd had nothing to eat.

Jessica did recover for a few days, but she wouldn't go far from the cave and she didn't eat much. I stayed beside her, feeling powerless.

Then I noticed she was lying down more and more. Her eyes were dull, and the wound on her neck had turned into an abscess. I knew we needed help. She needed a vet and an antibiotic injection like I'd been given. She needed a car to take her to the vet, and a caring person to do that for her. It was no good going to Joe. He hadn't got a car now, and Pam only had her bike. I thought about Karenza, but how could I get Jessica to her?

What would Ellen say if she knew?

I felt angry and desperate.

My angel had tried to tell me to let Jessica go. Was this what she had meant? Did I have to sit in this cold, dark wood and watch my best friend die? Jessica was more than my best friend. She was my love. And now she was all I had.

I lay down beside her and licked her face very gently.

'Do you think you might make it back to the camp-site?' I asked.

Jessica looked at me through half-closed eyelids.

'No,' she said. 'Just lie beside me and keep me warm.'

An icy wind was zigzagging through the wood. I patted Jessica with my paw, and she was limp, her tail stretched out on the ground. I set about washing her pink paws for her, licking the dried mud off them. She wanted to go outside and lie down in her favourite spot under an oak tree. Her legs were wobbly, but she made it, and I sat beside her, trying to place my body to shelter her from the bitter wind. I fluffed my fur out to keep myself warm.

The winter afternoon was darkening minute by minute. Jessica was weak now, her breathing rapid and shallow, but she managed to say one last word to me.

'You must let me go, Solomon. Go back and wait for Ellen.'

'How do you know that?' I asked.

'Your angel told me.'

I was devastated. I wanted to say thank you to Jessica. Thank you for all the fun times, and our beautiful kittens, and thank you for showing me the sea. I'll never forget you, Jessica.

But it was too late. Jessica was gone. She looked suddenly, utterly peaceful, her face curled around in a sort of smile.

I sat still and watched the light leaving her body like a haze of gold. Then I saw lights coming through the woods, golden lights and green lights low down on the forest floor, crowding in around the peaceful little cat. I moved back respectfully, and watched the tiny beings of light form a ring. The rays of light crisscrossed and made a dome-shaped lattice, which I recognised at once – the golden web.

I had passed through it when I was born, and now Jessica's buttercup light was rising, going through that sparkling web, leaving her body behind like an old coat. I watched the light melting away through the trees and the sky.

Broken hearted, I turned my attention to covering her body with leaves. I raked them up with my long paws and piled them over her as best I could.

My grief at losing Jessica was too painful to think about. I needed to be doing something positive before dark. I would run and run until I found the old badger hole again.

I was too upset to work out where to go. Through the night wood I ran, my body low to the ground, my tail down. I was aware of badgers, rabbits, and an owl, but I ignored them. Oblivious to the rain and the wind buffeting my fur, I ran and ran until I found myself on the high bridge that spanned the busy road.

Mesmerised by the headlights, I crouched with my head through the railings. If only one of those lorries would slow down, I'd have a chance. Jessica's words came back to me. 'Don't do it,' and she'd taken me to see the shining ocean. 'Because,' she'd said, 'you have to know what wonderful things are out there.'

I thought it through. Even if I did manage to make a spectacular leap onto the roof of a speeding lorry, I would have to cling on tightly for hundreds of miles, and it was raining. Or I might get blown off and killed on the road. What a waste of a cat like me. Memories of good things I had done started replaying in my mind. Being kind to little John. Walking into that hospital with my tail up. Playing penguins with Jessica.

Times were tough, but I didn't want to die. I wanted to finish my job, and my job was to love Ellen. I hurried back down the tarmac lane but soon realised I was exhausted, my paws were sore, and I was soaking wet. At the edge of a field was an old wooden shed. I crawled underneath it and slept for hours curled up in a hollow of dry earth.

In the morning I emerged to find a thin layer of snow lying over the fields. It made it difficult for me to hunt, and I was starving hungry, so I had nothing to eat. My energy was low as I headed towards the woods, and I couldn't remember which way to go. On and on I trotted, following winding animal tracks between the trees, and late in the day I was horrified to find I'd been going round in circles.

After a second night under the shed and still nothing to eat, I was desperate, and missing Jessica so much. Together we had survived and supported each other. Alone I began to feel I had no chance.

Just before dawn I heard the sound of another creature squeezing itself under the shed. I sat up quickly. I hadn't got the strength to fight or even defend myself. In the grey-pink light of sunrise I could see the shape of a badger, and to my surprise he came right up to me. He stood looking at me with wise old eyes.

I hadn't forgotten how to be polite so I stretched my head towards him, and we touched noses. I smelled him and, miracle of miracles, it was the old badger from the copse. I'd worked hard to make friends with those badgers, and now, in my hour of need, the old fellow had come out in the snow and found me. He wasted no time but turned around and set off through the fields. He turned just once to make sure I was following, and I was, our paws crunch-crunching over the frozen snow. He had come to lead me home.

The badger hole felt surprisingly warm and welcoming as I crawled in out of the snow. I could still smell Jessica on the floor where she had slept next to me, and a tuft of her fur clung to the dried moss. It must have come from her tummy, for it was pure white and soft. It looked like a delicate white moth in the dark hole. I lay down with my nose touching it, my paws stretched over the empty place where she had been. Where was she now? Jessica had shared lots of wisdom and fun with me but she'd never mentioned the spirit world. Had her memory of it been blanked? Was she there now? Could she see me there in our old refuge, hungry and grieving?

Then I thought of our tabby and white kitten I had loved so much. She'd be a cat now. I wished I could find her. I wished she would magically appear at the badger hole, all fluffed out, her eyes shining like lamps in the shadowy wood.

I had lost everything.

That first night alone in the badger hole was endlessly dark. I had only my memories.

Ellen used to read me stories when she was a child. I knew them all by heart and most had happy endings. Ellen would read faster and faster, her eyes alight, racing through the scary bits so that she could read the last page with a smile. As she got older the stories were longer and deeper, and one day she showed me a book called *The Diary of Anne Frank*, about a girl who had to hide away for years during the war. Like me, she was in a desperate situation, but every day she wrote it down in a diary. It made her feel better, and it helped people to understand, years later, what she had been through and how she had coped.

I remembered that book, and the sad girl on the cover. If I was able to write, then I would keep a diary now. I'd start today, and it would go something like this.

THE DIARY OF A DESPERATE CAT

I am all alone now and still sleeping in the badger hole. I'm in there most of the day as it's so cold. Today there is more snow whirling across the landscape. It piles higher and higher around my hole. My dinner is a small mouse, which I had been saving, and when I want a drink I lick some of the cold snow. My body is so thin that my ribs hurt when I lie down. Even my paws, which used to be soft and glossy, look bony and rough.

A fox comes by in the night and sticks his pointed nose right into my hiding place. The snow crystals on his whiskers glisten in the moonlight, and his eyes gleam as he looks in at me. I am too weak to fight, but the memory of Jessica confronting Paisley gives me courage. I puff myself up, flatten my ears and yowl ferociously. I smell the fox's musky breath. I attack his surprised face with claws of steel. He backs away. But he doesn't go. He skulks around, pacing to and fro, always looking at me with that rusty stare. He's hungry too. I crouch in the hole, glaring back at him, but the energy of being constantly on guard is draining me. I can read the fox's mind. He is waiting. And when I am weak, he will have me.

The fox sits down like a dog, watching me. His fur is in perfect condition, fiery red-gold and white. He's a creature of the wood, and he doesn't go hungry. He doesn't give up and lie in a hole with only his memories, like I am doing. In a way he's teaching me something.

I glance at the tiny white tuft of Jessica's fur. And I can hear her sweet voice in my head, and she's saying, 'It's no good just sitting there. You've got to go at him.

Be a dragon.'

I don't know where the strength is coming from but suddenly I am on fire. I charge out at the fox, right up to him. I scream at him and slash his nose with a paw made of iron. Again. And again. He yelps like a puppy. He turns and runs away. I stand there like the king of the wood.

It is morning now, and I've been awake all night watching for the fox. Hunger echoes through my body, but I so need to sleep in the morning sun. I am very, very lonely. I want Ellen. I want Jessica. I want the amber velvet cushion. I must be the coldest cat in the world, and the saddest.

Another day dawns.

The snow is melting now, and at midday the sun shines for a while. I venture out looking for food and find a crust of white bread that a bird has dropped. It is mouldy but I eat every single crumb. I go to look at the caravan. Will Ellen be there? In my mind I hear her sweet voice cry out my name and welcome me back. But the door is closed, the curtains drawn over every window, and there is tape over the cat flap. Sadness fills my being and I mooch about, my tail down, hoping to find something that will comfort me. Underneath, behind one of the wheels, I discover a very old dead mouse that Jessica had stashed there. Too exhausted to eat it, I carry it back to the badger hole in my mouth.

It will do for my breakfast if nothing else turns up. In the evening I can see the sunset between the trees and I watch for Jessica's star. It is there like a bright spirit shining in the twilight. I watch it rising behind the ash trees until I fall asleep.

It is moonlight outside and I can hear music and lots of footsteps coming down the lane. Something is different. I peer outside and see a lantern bobbing above the hedge. The music gets louder. I sit up. I remember that song. 'Silent Night, Holy Night'. Ellen used to sing that. Perhaps it is Christmas. Oh I loved Christmas. I used to get given a catnip mouse and a ball with a little bell inside. Jessica and I had one each and we played for hours. Then Jessica would shred all the wrapping paper and drag it under the sofa. I try to go to sleep, but in the middle of the night I hear the church bells ringing.

Another morning, another dawn, and it is frosty. Yes, it must be Christmas Day. I know because I hear those bells ringing again and the sound of carols being sung. And the distant village smells of roast potatoes. I used to get given a plate of chopped-up turkey with gravy. But this Christmas is the worst week of my life. Surely a cat shouldn't be all alone on Christmas Day? I'm getting angry. And where is my angel?

The day passes into night. Then morning. The hunger is deep and painful now. I am listless and weak, but I am still managing to wash. It's not fun because my fur is coming out. It's all over the place in the badger hole, and I've got some bare patches on my back and along my tail. Today the weather is still and I could go out, but I can't be bothered. I'd rather lie in here and die.

Where IS that angel? I close my eyes and purr for a while, and think hard about my angel. What did she look like? I begin to visualise the haze of shimmering light, I imagine the tingle of her stardust through my fur, I listen for her voice, and suddenly she is there. She has been there all the time; I just haven't been using my psi sense.

'Please help me,' I say to her. 'I'm dying. And I'm only a young cat.'

There is a silence. My angel is sending me energy and love. But it's not helping my wretched cold and starving body. It's not healing my troubled mind. Then she answers, and she says something I did not expect.

'You must help yourself, Solomon.'

She says no more. I lie there, angry, processing this information. Help myself indeed. But I'm a smart cat, and maybe I can figure out what to do. I can't do a big thing. But I can do a small thing. I'll do it. I'll stop this diary of self-pity and help myself. I'm going to start meowing, as long as I can, for as long as I have to.

CHAPTER
ELEVEN

IF CATS COULD CRY

At first the meows I did were a bit modest, but once I got into it, they were LOUD. I tried to make them more like a cry than a yowl. I sent the cry echoing through the winter landscape, into the caravans and the cottages and the lanes. Now and again I paused to listen.

I heard footsteps. Someone far away was pit-patting down the lane, coming closer, stopping. Someone had stopped to listen. I meowed even louder, trying to put hope into my voice. I heard heavy breathing and the thump of feet in the copse. Someone had scrambled over the wall and through the brambles.

I meowed faster to encourage the person.

'Where are you?' called a voice. 'Pussy cat?'

Meow. Meow.

'Are you up a tree? Down a tin mine? Come on where are you? I haven't climbed over that hedge for nothing you know.'

I knew that kind voice. It was Karenza. Her black boots came scrunching through the copse and stopped. She was looking around for me. I managed to stand up on my wobbly legs, and I just remembered how to put my tail up.

'Oh you poor, poor cat,' she gasped when she saw me. She came gently towards me. 'Will you let me pick you up?'

Would I let her! It was heaven to be in someone's arms again and feel a warm coat and hear a heartbeat. I purred and purred as if I would never stop.

Inside Karenza's cottage a bright fire was burning. She put me down on a sumptuous rug right next to it, and the warmth soaked into me. It was heavenly. Karenza seemed to know I was too weak to cope with the other cats and she shooed them into the kitchen and shut the door. She brought me a dish of Whiskas rabbit.

'Nothing wrong with your appetite,' she said as I tucked in. Afterwards I was too exhausted to wash. Feeling warm and safe, I stretched out by the fire to sleep. Before I drifted off, I heard Karenza talking on the phone.

'I've found Solomon,' she said and I heard a scream at the other end of the phone. 'He's here, and he's safe, and I'll take care of him until you come.'

My sleep was deep and blissful. Once in the night I awoke, surprised to find Karenza had put me in a round fluffy cat bed and taken me into her bedroom. She wasn't asleep but lying close to me with her hand on my back. I was so thin that when she stroked me her fingers seemed to be touching my bones. She was talking to me gently and her hand was full of stars. Healing stars. I began to purr, and the rhythmic purring and the stars mingled together through the night.

Karenza was a cat healer. She lived alone in the cottage and all her love was poured into looking after her cats. I was so lucky, I felt ashamed of my angry thoughts and the way I'd turned my back on my angel. But the pain of losing Ellen, and then Jessica, was overwhelming. I shuddered, and Karenza was there for me instantly, stroking and soothing, and telling me to go back to sleep.

In the morning Abby the vet turned up to see me.

'He'll be fine,' she said, after she'd given me a load of injections and told Karenza what they were. 'Worms, fleas, mange, cat flu jab and a vitamin boost. Just keep him warm, keep him away from the other cats until he's stronger, and feed him little and often.'

'He'll get lots of TLC,' said Karenza. 'And this afternoon he's getting a surprise.'

A surprise? I thought that might be a catnip mouse, but I wouldn't have the energy to play with it. All I wanted to do was sleep. Karenza carried my new fluffy bed to the fireside and I lay there gazing into the golden flames. I chose one flame that had a rim of sapphire blue, then orange, then white hot in the middle. In my mind I walked through that white-hot door into the land of pure light, and Jessica was there, washing her pink paws.

She looked beautiful and perfect, but far away where I couldn't reach her.

My angel came, and she said, 'You must heal in body and soul, Solomon. It will take a long time, so be patient with yourself. Now go back to sleep.'

I did, feeling like the warmest cat in the world.

In late afternoon when the winter sun was filling the cottage with beams of gold, I heard a car pull up outside. I heard feet running up the path.

'You wait till you see who this is, Solomon.' Karenza winked as she swept past me to answer the door.

She opened it, and there stood my Ellen.

If cats could cry, I'd have cried with happiness. I stepped out of the fluffy bed, and my legs felt stronger already. My tail went up by itself and I ran to greet my Ellen.

'Solomon,' she breathed, and picked me up. I licked the tears from her cheeks and purred.

'You darling, darling cat. And you're so thin. What have you been through?'

I wanted to tell her, but even if I'd had the words, I couldn't have spoken. It was too big, too painful to tell her about Jessica dying in the cold woods, the old badger leading me home, and the Diary of a Desperate Cat.

'Look at his fur,' Ellen said, smoothing me.

'The vet said it will grow back. She came out this

morning, and gave him some injections. She said he'll be fine.'

'Thank you, Karenza.'

Ellen gave Karenza a hug with one arm. She sat down by the fire with me on her lap. I noticed she looked better, there was a glow on her cheeks and she was wearing a beautiful sparkly scarf.

'I've left John with Pam,' she said. 'She's bringing him down in a short while.'

'So what's been happening?' said Karenza.

'John and I have been in a B & B,' explained Ellen. 'John hated it. But– I've just been to see Nick and he said we can have the caravan back. Joe left three weeks ago, he's gone up country to stay with his dad.'

'Was it drink?' Karenza asked.

'Yes. And his dad is getting him into rehab,' said Ellen. 'But I'm never going back with him, Karenza. Of course he'll have to see John. I'm much better on my own though, even in a B & B.'

Karenza grinned at her.

'Cats are better than men,' she said. 'I figured that out long ago. So when can you move back?'

'Next weekend,' said Ellen. 'Nick has kindly said he'll do a few repairs on the caravan, and he's going to put in a little wood burner, so we'll be cosy.'

'Well, I'll look after Solomon until you're ready.' Karenza gave my head a rub. 'Is that all right, Solomon?'

'He understands everything,' said Ellen. 'I just wish he could tell us where Jessica is.'

I sat up and gave the saddest meow I could muster. It came out as a wailing sound. Ellen and Karenza looked at each other. Ellen put both arms around me and looked right into my eyes.

'Has Jessica died, Solomon?' she whispered, and I did an even sadder meow and buried my head in her scarf because I couldn't bear the sadness.

'He's grieving,' said Karenza. 'I know a grieving cat when I see one. He'll need lots of time and love. I took him to bed last night and I'll do it again for him.'

'You're an angel. How can I ever thank you?'

John and Pam arrived next, and there were more tears. I was glad to feel John's small hand stroking me.

'Poor Solomon,' he kept saying. 'I missed you, Solomon.'

Pam had a big plastic bag, which she gave to Ellen.

'I brought you a present.'

'Oh Pam.' Ellen reached into the bag and took out the amber velvet cushion.

'I rescued it, after he'd chucked it out,' said Pam proudly. 'And I've washed it, and dried it, and even made it smell nice.'

'Wow!' Ellen buried her face in the cushion. 'It smells of lavender. Thank you, Pam. You're an angel.'

Another angel, I thought. Pam and Karenza. Two

earth angels. If I were a person instead of a cat, I would give them a bunch of roses each.

I was quite nervous about going into the caravan again. The memory of Joe's bad tempers would be in there, and the damp washing, and the way everything rattled in the wind.

After a week of Karenza's TLC, I was much better. My fur was growing back, my thin body was filling out again, my legs were strong and my tail was up most of the time. When the day came, Karenza carried me all the way up the lane inside her coat, and I knew my eyes were shining again as I looked around. High in the trees a song thrush was singing, and there were snowdrops and yellow celandines along the sides of the lane.

John had gone to school, but Ellen was there to welcome me home. She'd bought me a new basket and lined it with a cosy rug, and a new dish with food already in it for me. The caravan looked and smelled different. The best thing was the new stove full of a crackling fire, and it was *hot* in the caravan. It felt peaceful. I inspected everything, strutting around with my tail up. I went into John's bedroom and touched noses with his two teddy bears, then into Ellen's room and saw her slippers under the bed. I sniffed at Jessica's cupboard. It had been cleaned out and packed with boxes, but right in the corner I found Jessica's catnip mouse. I took it into my new basket, and settled down there, wondering what kind of life we would have here now, without Joe. 'There will be peace,' my angel had said.

She was right. Ellen, John and I were peaceful together. The caravan wasn't a house, but it was a cosy sanctuary, and there was no more shouting and screaming. Ellen spoke quietly to John and to me, and on wet afternoons the three of us would curl up together in front of the fire and Ellen would read John a story or play a game with him. We were as happy as we could be. I had something in common with John. Both of us were grieving, me for Jessica, and John for his daddy. At first John cried a lot and I was glad to be able to comfort him. I'd stretch myself out with my long paws over his chest, and my chin on his heart, purring and purring.

'You are SUCH a healing cat,' Ellen said to me once. 'But I know you still miss Jessica, don't you? You don't play like you used to.'

It was true. I didn't feel like playing. Jessica's death had left a big hole in my life, and I thought about her constantly. Ellen had a photo of Jessica's cheeky face on the wall near my basket, and I often sat gazing at it. I still loved her, and I kept her memory alive by remembering the fun times we had had, and all that she had taught me.

Cats are not brilliant at counting, so I don't know how long we lived there like this, peacefully in the caravan. Summer passed, and I was sleek and glossy again, and autumn rolled on into winter. John was growing bigger, and I knew that every two weeks Ellen took him to see his daddy, and both of them came back stressed and upset. But Joe never came to the caravan, and for that I was glad.

One bright winter morning, everything changed.

I was sitting on the caravan steps, washing my paws in the sunshine, when my angel appeared in a flare of white light. Usually I had to struggle to see her, but now she was sharply in focus and fizzing with stars.

'Be at your best, Solomon. Someone is coming, and he is very important. You must stay close to Ellen, and use all of your senses.'

'Who is it?' I asked, but already a gleaming black car was turning into the campsite, and my angel disappeared in a plume of light. I sat up and made myself look important, with stiff whiskers and fluffed-out fur.

The car drove quietly and carefully up to the caravan and stopped. A bailiff, I thought. Not again.

But a beautiful man got out and stood looking at the caravan. He was beautiful because of his aura, which I could see. It was huge and luminous with lots of turquoise and white, and the man reminded me of the sea. He had interesting blue eyes, which lit up when he saw me sitting on guard.

He didn't say, 'Hello puss,' like most did. He padded peacefully towards me and stretched out a chunky hand to stroke me. But first he asked permission, in a deep rumbly voice that I liked.

'May I stroke you? You are a beautiful friend.'

I did a special sound for him, a cross between a meow and a purr, and stood up on my hind legs to show him I wanted him to touch me. His touch was calm and loving, and he stroked me for several minutes before knocking at the caravan door. When he had knocked, he stepped back respectfully for Ellen to open it.

She stood there looking surprised and a bit anxious, wiping her hands on a flowery tea towel.

'Excuse me, I was baking,' she said.

The man didn't speak immediately and I saw he was looking at Ellen's long golden hair glinting in the winter sunshine.

'I'm Isaac Mead,' he said, and held out his hand. 'I'm a governor at John's school.'

Ellen shook hands with him, but she looked uneasy.

'Oh dear,' she said. 'Has John been playing up?'

'No – not at all. It's because of something that John said though, that's why I'm here.'

'You'd better come in.'

She took Isaac into the tiny kitchen, which smelled of warm cakes, and he sat down by the wood burner.

'Does this gorgeous cat have a name?' he asked.

'Solomon. Because he's so wise,' said Ellen, and I climbed onto her lap and sat there protectively, studying the deep blue of Isaac's eyes. He had a beard, and bits of it were grey, and he wore a duffel coat with toggles, which I wanted to play with.

'So what's this about?' Ellen's eyes were still wary. 'Is it bad news?'

'No my dear. No. You see the school is in rather a difficult situation. We've got the Christmas concert coming up, and now the pianist has had a heart attack. She won't be able to play for a long, long time, and when we told the children this in assembly they were really upset. Then your John put his hand up and said, "My mum can play the piano and she's brilliant."'

'Wow,' said Ellen, and her face glowed. 'Fancy him remembering. He was so young when we – we,' she hesitated, and Isaac just looked at her kindly and waited. 'We lost our home you see, and they took all our furniture, including my piano. So I haven't played for years.'

'Would you consider playing for the children?' Isaac asked.

Ellen couldn't seem to answer. She'd always said no as a child when her mother wanted her to perform.

There was a long silence. My angel had said Ellen missed her music, and that music would feed her soul. I knew Ellen had to say yes, and she wouldn't. So I decided to answer for her.

I looked at Isaac and gave a loud, firm meow. Then I batted Ellen's face with my paw, and meowed at her. I kept doing it until she smiled and said, 'OK, I'll have a go,' and I rubbed my head against her and purred.

'Perhaps you'd better bring Solomon,' smiled Isaac.

'I could. He's a very well behaved cat – and he loves music,' explained Ellen. 'Maybe he'd give me confidence. He always used to sit on top of the piano. He really loves Mozart.'

'The children would love him,' said Isaac. 'And John would be so proud of you.'

'I'd need to practise. There isn't room for a piano in here, even if I could afford one. I'm a single parent.'

'I've got a piano,' said Isaac. 'I'm afraid it hasn't been played for years, but it's a beauty – a grand. It's a bit dusty, like the rest of my place. I live alone you see, since my dear wife died of cancer …'

'Oh, I'm sorry,' Ellen said kindly. She put her slim hand on Isaac's arm, and tiny sparks danced in his aura.

'I'll go home now, and clear all my stuff off the top of it.' Isaac's eyes shone with enthusiasm. 'Then you can come down and practise. I promise not to listen. I'll be up a ladder putting a new roof on the barn. You can bring John. It would be good to have some life in the old place. It's just me and the mice at the moment.'

I meowed at Ellen again, and this time she responded.

'I'd … like that. I really would. Thank you, and I'd so appreciate you not listening! I've always been shy about performing.'

Isaac looked at her silently, nodding his head a little. His eyes glanced around the caravan, at the picture of Jessica, the bowl of oranges, the neatly stacked books and box of Lego, the cosy rugs and cushions.

'You've made a beautiful little home here,' he said, rather wistfully. His eyes looked at Ellen again, and suddenly I remembered meeting Jessica for the first time. As soon as I'd seen her challenging buttercup eyes, I'd fallen in love with her, and the love was forever.

Isaac was being quiet and courteous. But I knew a secret, even before he knew it. Isaac had fallen in love with Ellen.

On the night of the Christmas concert I was the proudest cat on the planet.

Ellen had bought me a special cat harness, with a lead, and she'd taken me into John's classroom. With the door firmly shut, I was set free and I knew exactly what to do. Tail up and purring I walked around loving the children, and they adored me. Then I showed them how I liked to sit on the piano while Ellen played. After a few of these sessions, I was allowed to go to the performance on a starry winter night.

Pam was assigned to look after me, and she sat squarely in the front row close to the piano, in her best red coat. The children were used to me by now, but they still buzzed with excitement when Pam put me firmly on top of the piano. I sat up smartly, looking at everyone.

'Please welcome our pianist, Ellen King,' said the headmaster, and everyone clapped. I was so proud of Ellen, I could have burst. She swept in, wearing a black velvet coat, with her golden hair swinging down her back. I lay down immediately and had eye contact with her as she sat down at the piano.

She began to play the Christmas music with great energy and love, and everyone listened. Ellen kept glancing at me, and I knew I was helping her. No one except me knew how nervous she'd been. The music helped her too. Once she had started, she was happy. The audience and the children stood up to sing and I really loved the sound they made. I watched Isaac and he was gazing raptly at Ellen.

The children did a play, and John was a shepherd. He had a tea towel on his head and a stick he had cut from the hedge. When the play was over and everyone had finished clapping, I was allowed to go on stage. I strutted on with my tail up and all the children wanted to stroke me. I wanted to inspect the toy sheep that John was carrying, and I touched noses with it. Then I thought I ought to see what was in the crib they were all looking at, so I climbed up and touched noses with the plastic doll who was in there. Everyone laughed, but I didn't see what was so funny.

'Well done, Solomon,' said the headmaster. He was

leaning on the piano, so I ran back and touched noses with him, and the children laughed and laughed.

Ellen's eyes were sparkling as she started to play again, and everyone sang lustily, a song about a figgy pudding.

'Eee,' said Pam, as we all walked home under the stars. 'That were the best night I've had in years. And that cat was the star of the show.'

The following morning Ellen's mobile phone kept ringing; and I noticed she was smiling a lot and singing the 'figgy pudding' song as she worked. She and John had decorated a small Christmas tree and the baubles fascinated me. I sat looking at a pink one, intrigued to see a tiny cat inside it who looked like me.

'That's you, Solomon,' said John, and he appeared beside the cat in the bauble. 'And me. It's a reflection.'

I stared at it, and when I moved the tiny cat moved too, and I could see Ellen in there hanging decorations in the window – paper snowflakes that she and John had made together. I patted the bauble with my paw, hoping to get it down on the floor and chase it. But Ellen spoke to me, firmly.

'No, Solomon, please don't play with the Christmas tree,' and I meowed back and sat still to show her I understood.

'It's a good thing Jessica isn't here,' said John. 'She'd trash it, wouldn't she Mummy?'

I looked sadly at Jessica's photograph. A year had passed and I still missed her so much.

I moved round to inspect the reflections on the other side of the bauble; the trees in the copse, the caravans, the entrance gate, all in miniature. Isaac's shiny black car was arriving. He came so often now that I knew the sound of his car. I jumped down and ran to the door with my tail up.

Ellen looked pleased, and so did John.

We all ran out to meet Isaac, who got out of the car a bit sheepishly, with the biggest bunch of flowers I'd ever seen. Pink and red, yellow and white, inside a cone of crackly cellophane which Jessica would have loved.

Ellen's cheeks glowed as Isaac thrust the bouquet into her hands. I noticed she had done her hair nicely, tied back with a floaty red scarf, and her eyes were alive again, the way they had been when she was a child.

'WOW. Are those for me, Isaac?' she asked.

'They're from all of us at the school, to say thank you,' Isaac said. He hesitated, then leaned forward and gave Ellen a kiss on her cheek. 'And that's a warm thank you from me, my dear. We all enjoyed your playing so much. It was *marvellous*.'

And when he said the word 'marvellous' in his rumbly voice, something amazing happened which only I could see. An angel appeared in a flare of gold, a new angel who I'd never seen before. Her robe fizzed with points of light and it swirled around Ellen and Isaac, wrapping them in stars. It electrified my fur from head to tail as it swished over me. I looked at John. Had he seen it too? His eyes were full of its light, but he stayed silent, and I could read his thoughts. He did see it, but he wasn't going to say so.

'These are wonderful flowers.' Ellen buried her face in them. 'The perfume! And the colours! I ... I've never had such a bouquet.'

Isaac smiled, looking down at her, his eyes radiating kindness.

'The first of many, I hope,' he said, and rubbed his chunky hands together. 'Brr, it's cold. I'll be glad to get in by the fire. Is your little stove going?'

'Not yet.' Ellen said. 'I had trouble lighting it this morning.'

'I'll do it for you ... in return for a coffee,' said Isaac eagerly.

'And will you make a Lego model with me?' John asked. 'Please?'

'When I've lit the fire ... if that's OK with your mum.'

'That would be brilliant,' said Ellen. 'I'll put the kettle on.'

I glanced across at Pam's caravan and she was watching out of her window with a big smile on her face. She stuck her thumbs up and winked at me. Isaac sat on the floor with the stove doors open, twisting bits of news-paper and popping them in around the kindling. He lit a match and sat there blowing and twiddling paper until orange flames were roaring up the flue. I rubbed myself against him, purring, walking round and round him, over his lap and stretching up to kiss his nose and feel his beard brushing my whiskers.

I buzzed with excitement when Ellen gave me the crackly cellophane from the flowers. She put it on the floor and I pounced and skidded and scrunched it. I wanted to hear Isaac laugh, and he did, and the caravan shook with his happy laughter. His eyes crinkled and his face went red, and Ellen and John were laughing at me too.

We had a great afternoon. John settled down with his Lego and Ellen sat peacefully talking to Isaac. He did a lot of attentive listening, and I could see him looking at the ballet shoes hanging on the wall. When he stood up to go home, he touched the pink silk ribbon with one finger.

'Who's the dancer?' he asked.

Ellen blushed. 'Me,' she said. 'I used to do ballet. I loved it. Ballet and music were … were my passion.'

Isaac looked down at her with deepening interest.

'Well,' he said, stroking his beard thoughtfully. Slowly he put his hand into his pocket and took out a glossy leaflet. 'It so happens that this came through my door today. It's the Hall for Cornwall programme in Truro. Have you been there?'

'No. Never,' said Ellen. 'We couldn't possibly afford to go.'

'They're doing a ballet. *Swan Lake.* I … don't suppose you'd like to come with me, would you Ellen?'

Ellen stared at him, her mouth open, her eyes full of light.

'I'd love to,' she whispered, and looked at John. 'But …'

I rubbed against Isaac's legs to show my approval, and John said, 'You go Mummy. Pam will look after me, and Solomon.'

'I'll fetch you, and bring you home,' said Isaac, 'and I can pay for the tickets. It would be my pleasure to take you.'

I had to meow at Ellen twice before she said, 'Yes … yes, I'd love that Isaac.'

'Right.' Isaac got up and put on his duffel coat. 'I shall go home now and book them this instant.'

The minute he'd gone, Pam came bustling over.

'Eee,' she said, 'look at them flowers.'

'He's invited me to the ballet, at the Hall for Cornwall in Truro,' said Ellen.

'Eee …' Pam sat down and I saw tears in her eyes. She leaned forward and whispered, 'I reckon Isaac Mead fancies you, Ellen.'

Ellen went red. 'Maybe he does,' she said.

'He's a lovely man,' said Pam, 'a lovely man, and so lonely since his wife died. He's all on his own in that big farmhouse like a pea in a drum.'

'But Pam ...' said Ellen. '*What* am I going to wear?'

'He won't care,' said Pam. 'He'll probably turn up in his old duffel coat. Anyway, you are going, aren't you? And you know I'll look after John and Solomon.'

'Thanks Pam, you're a star.'

It was the first of many times when Isaac came and took Ellen out, and I watched her slowly coming alive again, singing and making things, and reading stories to John. And I enjoyed the evenings with Pam. It seemed that everything had come right for me, if only Jessica had been there to share the cosy life we now had.

CHAPTER
TWELVE

THE DIARY OF A STAR CAT

I only had one terrible fear in my life. The cat basket. There were bad memories of being taken away from Jessica that day. How it felt to be imprisoned, to have to fight so fiercely for my freedom, had left scars in my mind. One day Ellen tried to take me to the vet, and when I saw that cat basket I ran away and hid in the same old badger hole. I stayed there all day until dark and I heard the anxiety in Ellen's voice as she called me, banging my dish with a spoon. So I went home to a warm welcome, and the cat basket was nowhere to be seen.

The next day Abby the vet came to see me and gave me what she called a booster jab.

'How old is he now?' she asked, stroking me under my chin.

'He must be seven,' said Ellen. 'I don't know why he's got those grey hairs round his face. Seven isn't old for a cat, is it?'

'It's middle age,' said Abby. 'But don't forget Solomon went through a major trauma and it may be that he'll age quicker.'

'And we don't know what happened,' said Ellen, 'or what he'd been through when he was a kitten. And I do think he's still grieving for Jessica. He lies and gazes at her photograph.'

'Well, he's in good condition anyway,' said Abby. 'His coat's beautiful.'

'I want him to be as strong as he can,' said Ellen. 'We've got another huge change coming and I don't want him to get upset.'

The words rang in my head. Another huge change! What could that be? I was settled now, even without Jessica my life was as good as it got. I didn't want another upheaval. Especially if it involved Joe. Or the cat basket.

My anxiety led me to seek out refuges again. I went down the lane to see Karenza. I made friends with Pam's dog who was smaller than me, and I was allowed into her caravan for a cuddle and a titbit. The old badger hole was my private sanctuary, and the tuft of white fur from Jessica's coat was still there. It comforted me as I slept with my nose touching it. Inside the hole I listened to every car that came down the lane, and if one slowed down and turned into the campsite, I was instantly awake and nervous. Was it Joe? Was it a bailiff?

One day in early summer when the copse was full of bluebells and pink campion, I heard the sound of Isaac's car turning in. I loved Isaac, so I got up, stretched and dashed through the tall flowers and over the wall to greet him.

He was standing outside the caravan with his arms full of empty cardboard boxes. Ellen came out and he put the boxes down and gave her a big bear hug. She hugged him back and her aura glowed like a sunset.

'I'm here,' said Isaac, 'and this is the best day of my life.'

'And mine,' Ellen said, gazing up at him.

I ran to them meowing, my tail up.

'Here he is. Hello, Solomon,' said Isaac, and picked me up. I purred and made a fuss of him.

'He loves you,' Ellen said, 'he always comes running doesn't he?'

In the caravan I sat on the sunny windowsill and wondered why Ellen and Isaac were taking everything down from the shelves and packing it into boxes. The kitchen china went in, then Ellen's books and her ballet shoes. I turned to look at Jessica's photograph, and it had gone. It was a shock. I stood in the space and meowed at Ellen.

'Don't worry, Solomon, Jessica's photo is packed. It's quite safe, darling, and you shall see it again very soon.'

Ellen had always explained stuff to me, but just lately I hadn't been listening. With a growing sense of alarm I watched her dragging two big bags out of a cupboard and packing John's clothes and teddies into them. When had this happened before? On that terrible day when I'd

207

been abandoned.

Surely it wasn't happening again!

I got more and more spooked. My fur began to bristle, and I sat stiffly, watching Isaac carrying the boxes to the car.

The caravan looked bare, as if no one lived there.

Ellen went outside, and came in with the cat basket.

I took one look at it and ran as if someone had set fire to my tail.

'Oh no!' I heard Ellen cry. 'Solomon!'

I shot up my favourite ash tree in the copse and sat there hidden by the green summer leaves. Ellen and Isaac were calling for me, but I ignored them. I watched the sunlight flickering on the leaves as they moved in the breeze. I heard the scream of the seagulls flying overhead, and I remembered the shining sea.

It had been so long since I'd talked to my angel. Had I become a boring switched-off old cat? I focused on the light, remembered the silver stars, and listened beyond the wind in the trees. And from somewhere among those sounds my angel's voice began to talk to me.

'All is well, Solomon. You must go back,' she said. 'Ellen wants to take you to live with Isaac, and this is good for her and for you. You will be quite safe in the cat basket. I will watch over you. Stay calm and this time nothing will hurt you.'

'I can't,' I said. 'I just can't go inside that basket.'

'You can, Solomon. Isaac has a lovely home where you will be free and happy. It's time to move on.'

I clambered down from the tree, thinking about what she'd said. In my heart I wanted to be with Jessica again. I decided to go to the badger hole, one last time, and sit close to the tiny white tuft of Jessica's fur. Then maybe I would try to go home.

Sensing a movement inside the hole as I approached, I sat down to watch. A bird was in there! A robin. I watched him hopping about and saw his head move to peck something. I heard the burr of his wings as he flew past. In his beak was Jessica's tuft of white fur. He was going to line his nest with it.

My last link with Jessica was gone.

With my tail down I padded slowly homeward through the copse, just looking at the ground in front of me. I was tired of life, and deeply grieving, and afraid.

When I got to the caravan I was surprised to see Karenza sitting on the grass with Ellen. Normally I would have run to them with my tail up, but I couldn't.

Ellen gave a cry, 'Oh HERE he is! Solomon …'

I didn't go to her but crept right under the caravan into the dark and crouched there.

'What's wrong with him? He must be hurt, or sick,' said Ellen, and she lay on her tummy and tried to coax me out. I felt too numb to move. 'Please Solomon,' she pleaded, 'I love you so much. I won't leave you ever again. Please come out.'

'Let me try,' said Karenza, and she crawled under the caravan and lay beside me. She looked into my eyes for a long time, and gently put her hands on me. I felt a warm glow from them, and I remembered that touch, how she had taken me into her bed and healed me through the night.

'I need to spend some time with him, Ellen,' she said. 'Can you hang in there?'

'OK, I'll just sit here quietly.'

Karenza began to talk to me by telepathy, which made it so easy. The thoughts were rippling to and fro between us. Instead of lecturing me, Karenza asked me questions, deep questions that needed to be answered.

'What is it you want to tell me, Solomon?'

'I want to go with Ellen, but I can't. I can't go in that cat basket.'

'What happened to make you so afraid?'

'I was … kidnapped … by a family and they were going to take me to London, and call me Fred.'

'So what did you do?'

'I … I went crazy, and hurt myself. I made my paws bleed, and my nose. I was covered in blood. I had to make them let me out.'

Karenza paused and sent me a whoosh of love from her hands. It was better than the amber velvet cushion. I sensed her tuning in to my deepest secrets.

'That must have been hard for you, Solomon. You don't like fighting do you? You're such a loving cat.'

What she said, and the way she said it, gave me such peace to know that a human understood. I wanted to purr, but instead, I sort of cried like a human in little squeaks and growls, and the sound travelled right through me, carrying the pain away. Karenza stayed with me, and I saw that Ellen had crawled under the caravan too and her beautiful eyes were looking at me like two big lamps. I reached out a paw to her to show I cared.

Then Karenza asked me about Jessica, by telepathy, and I was able to tell her everything. It was such a relief. I even told her about the robin flying off with the tuft of white fur.

Each time I told her something and she listened, I felt lighter, and better. The dark space under the caravan seemed full of the haze of stardust. I began to feel like a new cat.

I purred and stretched. I kissed Ellen on the nose. Then I walked out into the sunshine and the two women crawled after me, their hands and clothes grubby from the dust. I sat on Ellen's lap and purred while Karenza told her everything.

'He's a very traumatised cat,' she said, and then added something which made me feel a whole lot better. 'And he must never be expected to go in a cat basket again, Ellen. He can't, and he needs you to understand that.'

Ellen was silent.

'It's my fault,' she said eventually. 'I should never have left him that time.'

'Solomon's forgiven you. Haven't you, Solomon?' said Karenza, and I purred louder, put my paws around Ellen's neck, and gave her a cat-hug.

'Look at him. He's giving me so much.' Ellen rubbed her cheek against my head. 'But how are we going to get him down to Isaac's place? The caravan is all locked up now and I've given the keys to Nick. We've officially moved out.'

Karenza's eyes gleamed and she rummaged in the bag she always carried over her shoulder. It had a fabric cat on it with eyes made of tiny beads. She took out something that looked like a sock, and let me sniff it. It smelled of one of her cats.

'This is a new kind of cat harness,' she said. 'He'll be quite safe in it. And we can walk him down to Isaac's place. That's the natural way for a cat to travel, and he won't be frightened at all.'

'It's five miles, Karenza, and look at the time.'

'I don't bother about time,' said Karenza. 'I'll come with you, and we'll go across the fields. I know the way. And we'll take turns carrying Solomon if he doesn't want to walk.'

'That's wonderful of you – thanks,' said Ellen, taking the sock thing from Karenza. I let her slip it over my head and gently pull my front paws through the two arm holes. It was comfortable and I felt OK in it. Karenza clipped a long lead onto it, and I rolled around on my back, playing with it for a few moments of being silly.

Then we set off into the golden evening, walking west. We walked through bluebell woods and along lanes perfumed with clouds of white flowers, through a village and over a bridge. It was a long way.

'He loves it,' said Ellen. 'He's had his tail up all the way.'

On top of a hill we stopped for a rest, and the two women drank from bottles of water as we watched the sun going down.

'That's Isaac's place.' Ellen pointed to a huddle of buildings in the valley below. 'It's an old farmhouse. You'll love it, Solomon.'

I hoped it was going to be OK.

Seeing Ellen so happy with Isaac, I was a bit jealous. They both loved me and gave me everything I needed, but I still missed Jessica. Sometimes I wanted her so much that I ached inside.

Isaac's place was a roomy farmhouse with deep stone windowsills lined with cushions. And it had STAIRS! I did try to play on my own, and everyone encouraged me. John ran up and downstairs dragging a catnip mouse on a string, and I enjoyed that game.

Isaac had a magnificent piano and I took to lying on his lap and purring while we both soaked up the beautiful music Ellen loved to play. I grew to trust Isaac totally, and I could see that Ellen and John had a happy life with him.

The garden was a wild tangle of overgrown shrubs festooned with honeysuckle and bramble. Underneath was a network of green tunnels, used by various wild creatures. Exploring on my own was spooky, but I persevered, and one day I made an amazing discovery.

I found a gate overgrown with ivy, and beyond it was a secret path winding between tall pink foxgloves. It looked mossy and inviting, and as I sat staring at it, I suddenly felt that Jessica was with me. She would have gone straight down there. My fur started to bristle with excitement. I squeezed under the gate and trotted down the path, not knowing what I was going to find.

The grass was hot and bees were buzzing, but there was a rhythmic swishing sound. It changed suddenly to a majestic roar as the path opened onto a rocky hillside, and there before me was the sea.

Now I knew where to go to think about Jessica.

I selected a warm rock and sat on it for a long time, gazing at the blaze of sunlight on the water. I watched enormous sparkles pirouetting at the edges, dancing away and then massing together. It seemed to me that the sea was full of angels, and if I stared for long enough

I would see them. I never did, but if I closed my eyes and imagined that mass of silver sparkles, I saw my own angel clearly.

Time passed. Autumn, Christmas, and spring. Another year, and then another. I lost track of how many, but I was aware that my body wasn't quite as agile as it used to be. My legs were stiff in the mornings, and I wasn't so good at climbing trees. But I still loved to explore and make friends with badgers and catch mice when I could be bothered.

One day when I was exploring the wild cliff-side beyond the garden, my angel told me to listen. I did, but heard only the seagulls and the wind in the bushes, and the zee-zeet of grasshoppers.

'No,' she said. 'Listen deep.'

I focused on the deep dark places under the thick canopy of gorse and heather, and listened again, picking up a brittle whisper of something moving in there. Then I heard a squeak that might have been a meow, and my hackles went up. After what happened to Jessica, I didn't want to meet a feral cat.

I sat quietly and waited.

Minutes later I heard the squeak again, and a delicate golden face peeped at me from the undergrowth. It didn't look or feel threatening so I meowed back. A small ginger cat crept out and ran to me eagerly. She was terribly thin and her eyes looked haunted. We touched noses, and my bristling fur subsided. I lay down and she snuggled next to me. I started to lick her ginger fur to reassure her, and I could feel her bones, she was so thin. I sensed her loneliness and hunger. She didn't seem able to talk to me, but I knew she was in trouble, so I encouraged her to follow me. I led her along the path, under the gate and into the garden, right onto the patio outside the kitchen door where Ellen had put my lunch.

I shared it with the tiny ginger cat, and she ate ravenously. When she was satisfied she sat with me on the warm stones, and washed her skinny little paws.

But when Ellen came out of the back door, the little cat's eyes went huge and black with alarm. She took off so fast that her claws left scratch marks in the dust. She vanished into the bushes and we didn't see her again for several days.

Then she returned, watchful and slinking, but she wouldn't eat until Ellen put the dish further away from the house.

'She's a wild cat,' Ellen said. 'Not an old softie like you, Solomon.'

Old? Me? I suppose I was getting old now, for a cat. We'd been at Isaac's place for years and John was a big boy now, going to school on the bus with a stack of books in his bag. He was learning to play the guitar, and he liked me to sit on his bed with him while he practised. I didn't know exactly how old I was.

Ellen gave the little ginger cat a name, Lulu.

'It gives her an identity,' she said.

'You'll never tame a wild cat,' said Isaac. 'But let her come if she wants to. Poor little mite.'

But Ellen and John were determined. Every day they put out extra food for Lulu. At first they put it near the bushes where she felt safe. I spent time in the bushes with Lulu, washing her and purring, and sometimes if she felt safe she cuddled up to me and slept.

'Why are you so scared?' I asked her one day. 'Ellen is kind and lovely. She'd never hurt you.'

'I've never seen one of those humans before,' she said. 'I didn't know what they were. They are huge and they look so scary.'

'Where did you come from, Lulu?' I asked.

She sighed and looked sad.

'I was born in the bushes where you found me,' she said. 'And I had a mum, ginger like me, and a sister too. She was ginger and white and used to play with me. But one day our mum led us across the road because she thought we would find more to eat over there. The cars were coming so fast, savage they were. I hung back, but Mum and my sister tried to run across and they got killed. So I was left alone.'

I felt so sad for Lulu. I knew how painful it was for her.

'You try to make friends with a human,' I said. 'Then you'll have a happy life like me.'

'I never will,' Lulu said. 'Never. Never.'

It was no good trying to tell her.

But Ellen had a plan.

She started sitting outside in a chair, sitting quite still, and eventually Lulu got used to her being there and came to eat from the dish Ellen put out for her. Gradually Ellen moved the dish and the chair closer together until Lulu was eating her food within touching distance. While she was eating Ellen talked to her softly, sometimes she actually sang to her, and I could see Lulu flicking her ears to listen. If Ellen moved, Lulu looked up at her and hissed like a snake.

I helped by rubbing myself around Ellen's legs or draping myself over her lap to show Lulu it was OK. One day the dish was so close that Ellen reached down and gently rubbed Lulu's back while she was eating. This went on for weeks and weeks, but it was Isaac who finally tamed Lulu. She couldn't seem to resist his rumbly voice and the calm touch of his big hands. She even rolled on her back and played with his shoelaces.

Then one chilly day in autumn, Isaac gently eased his hands around Lulu and picked her up. He put her on his lap and let go. Lulu lay there, looking surprised. She looked at me and I climbed up there with her and showed her how to lie and listen to Isaac's slow heartbeat, and she did.

John and Ellen stood motionless, watching with smiles on their faces. It was a moment of magic, and it changed Lulu's wretched lonely life forever.

Months later, Lulu was as daft as me, rolling over and purring, and climbing on laps. I taught her everything about living in a house, and we even played on the stairs. She made a lot of mistakes, but the wonderful thing about humans is that they are so forgiving and kind.

I knew Ellen had forgiven me for not bringing Jessica back, but I had never forgiven myself. Befriending Lulu had been good for me. It was my way of saying thank you to the people who had rescued me – Karenza, and Pam, and Abby the vet. And I was grateful to Isaac for sharing his lovely home with us.

I was a lucky cat now.

The years rolled on, happy and peaceful, and then I started getting old. My bones ached, and I was stiff. I could still put my tail up, but I didn't want to play. I didn't go to look at the sea any more. I just wanted to lie by the fire and sleep.

One day my back legs wouldn't work any more, and I had to drag myself around.

Abby came to see me with her vet's bag in her hand. She picked me up and felt me all over.

'He's got arthritis,' she told Ellen. 'But he's a very old cat now isn't he?'

'He's twelve,' said Ellen. 'John was two when we found Solomon. He just appeared on our lawn in a thunderstorm. It was midsummer night. He was a skinny little kitten covered in car oil.'

'Hmm.' Abby was feeling my tummy. 'That's a good age for a cat. I suspect he's got internal problems too. We might be able to do something but you'd have to bring him in.'

I looked at Ellen and she had tears in her eyes.

'No,' she said. 'I don't want to put him through all that now he's old. I'd rather just keep him here and love him and let him go.'

I looked at Ellen with gratitude. She loved me, but she was going to let me go. I was ready now. Ready to go home.

'A wise lady,' said Abby. 'But call me, Ellen, if you want me to help him. You know what I mean.'

THE DIARY OF A STAR CAT

I am writing this diary again as a gift to Ellen. I want her to know where I am going.

Because today I begin my journey to the stars.

Ellen has done the right thing. She doesn't want me to go to the vet and have surgery. She is going to love me, and let me go. Today she has put me on the amber velvet cushion in my favourite chair. She knows I can't walk any more. My back legs are weak. She is feeding me little spoonfuls of tasty food, but I don't really want it. I don't want to be in this old body any longer.

Thank goodness I can still purr. I can still open my eyes and see Ellen's lovely face. I can hear her voice talking to me and she is saying 'Thank you, Solomon. Thank you for being my cat. I'll always love you.' Some of the time Isaac is there too, and his touch on my fur is soothing and blissful. And John is there with me. He's nearly a man now. He wants to cry over me but he won't, so he sits beside me playing heavenly music on his guitar. He goes on playing into the night.

It is morning and Pam comes to see me, and she cries and cries. Then she tells me stories about Jessica, and the Christmas concert, and the time I visited Ellen in hospital. When she is gone Ellen tells me I am a star. A star cat. It reminds me to think about stars. I imagine the blaze of sunlight on the sea that Jessica showed me. I go to sleep and dream of the dance of silver stars and how I believed that the shining sea was full of angels, if only I could see them.

Another day and I am still on the amber velvet cushion. I'm sleeping most of the time. Today I have a surprise visitor, and it is Joe. 'Don't worry, Solomon,' Ellen whispers. 'I'm not going back with Joe. He just wants to say goodbye.' I open my eyes. Joe looks different. He smells nice and his eyes are calm. He tells me he is sorry for the way he treated us, and I purr and reach out my paw to him to show I have forgiven him. Then I sleep on a silver bed in the silver stars that are drifting all around me.

It is night time, and only Ellen is with me, stroking and talking, and Lulu is sitting on the arm of the chair, watching me. I am glad I found Ellen another cat. I can hardly see her now because the silver stars are clustered around me. They are lifting me, like a magic carpet, and carrying me away into the blaze of light. I am floating faster and faster, but I can hear Ellen's beautiful voice, and I am still purring.

Ellen and Lulu are like faraway pictures now. I can see the amber velvet cushion with the body of a very old black cat lying on it. I hear Ellen saying, 'Goodbye Solomon. Darling cat.' I am flying now, through the glittering stars, there are thousands of them whizzing past me, and they are turning from silver into gold. At last, I see the angels, and I burst through the golden web as if I am a firework.

I have come safely home to the spirit world, to my idyllic valley where the grass is full of stars, and the rocks are like warmest velvet. I am a shining cat now, made of pure light, and it feels amazing. I sit up and gaze into the distance, and something is moving. A cat. Another cat. Dashing towards me with its tail up. It is a shining cat.

And it is Jessica.

READER'S EXTRAS

A NOTE ON TUXEDO CATS

A NOTE ON TUXEDO CATS

Solomon and Jessica were real cats who shared our home. Solomon actually lived until the grand old age of 23, and Jessica to 14. Both were Tuxedo cats with black coats and tails and a white chest and paws, looking as if they were wearing white shirts and dinner jackets.

In legend the first cat to arrive in the new world was a Tuxedo cat named Asgerd, who sailed to North America on a Viking ship. T.S. Eliot's Jellicle cat was a Tuxedo, and other famous Tuxedo cats include Felix the Cat, Tom Cat from Tom and Jerry, and Jess from *Postman Pat*. Both Sir Isaac Newton and William Shakespeare owned Tuxedo cats.

Research has proved that Tuxedo cats are more intelligent than other cats and more creative in the games they play. Tuxedo kittens open their eyes 24 hours earlier than other cats, and they are able to see infrared light. Tuxedo cats are super sensitive and will often go off to find the person they feel is their rightful owner, as Solomon does in the story.

THE REAL LIFE
SOLOMON

THE REAL LIFE SOLOMON

One midsummer night I was in bed listening to a thunderstorm when I heard loud persistent meowing. I got up and opened the window, and there, alone in the night, was a tiny wet kitten. He saw me and turned his meows up an octave. I ran downstairs and picked him up from the front lawn. He weighed almost nothing but his purr was immediate and powerful as he cuddled close to me. I woke my husband, and together we gave this scrap of a kitten a bath to remove the car oil from his fur, and discovered he was a tuxedo cat; black with a white bib and paws.

Nobody claimed him, so we kept him, and named him Solomon because he was so wise and loving. Right from the start he gave us intense eye contact and love. My husband had a heart problem, and Solomon knew. He would spread himself out over Ted's chest, stretch his paws across his heart, and purr so deeply that Ted could feel the vibration going into the depths of his heart. It seemed to be exactly the right frequency for the gentle healing he needed. Ted found it so comforting and we were sure it helped him recover.

That was just the beginning of Solomon's life as a healing cat. He didn't hang about waiting to grow up but went straight to the work he had come here to do – healing. Solomon would look intensely at everyone he encountered, visitors, neighbours, and children. He waited until they sat down and then homed in on them, always finding a place of pain, a knee, a shoulder, or an upset stomach; but so often it was the heart, and even if there wasn't a physical problem with it, that person would be suffering deep emotional pain, and Solomon knew. It got to the point where people didn't come to see us any more. They came to see the cat!

Solomon was always gracious and loving, but he had a quirky sense of humour which he used wisely. He would save it for times of tension or arguments in the family. He'd walk in with his tail up, look round, and decide 'Hey, you guys are getting too serious.' Then he would do something which had raised a laugh the last time he did it, like lying on his side and kicking the hearthrug, sliding all round it as if he was riding a bike.

Later in his life, we had a vineyard and shop, and Solomon loved to welcome customers. If he paid particular attention to someone, we invited them to sit down with him, and many people experienced healing and were moved to tears by the love from this beautiful cat. Solomon lived to the grand old age of 23. I loved him so much, and so I have written this book, *Solomon's Tale*, with him as the main character and narrator.

It seems that dear Solomon really was my lucky black cat!

THE
ORPHANED
KITTENS

THE ORPHANED KITTENS

One sunny day in mid-September I discovered four new born kittens under a potato plant in the garden. I watched from a distance as the mum cat, Minnie, trotted to and fro caring for her new children. Minnie was a feral cat, a pretty tabby with a sweet face. Over the summer we had tried to befriend her and she was beginning to trust us, sitting close sometimes, and enjoying the food we put out for her. With winter coming on we were concerned about how she would raise her family in the wild.

About a week later Minnie carefully moved her kittens, taking them deep into a thick hedge. Fortunately the weather was warm and dry, and four weeks later we were delighted to see the tiny kittens, three black and one tortie, happily playing in the morning sun at the edge of the hedge.

But one terrible afternoon Minnie was killed on the road. The car didn't stop, but the girl who was following it had the decency to come to our door. She had tried to rescue Minnie and was very upset. Thank you, whoever you were, because what you actually did was save the lives of Minnie's beautiful kittens who were now motherless and alone in the hedge. We worried about them all night and were relieved to see them emerge the next morning to have a go at lapping the 'kitty milk' I had mixed up for them.

It was impossible to catch them and, concerned for their well being, we rang the Cats Protection League. An angel called Margaret came straight over, bringing a cat trap, sachets of kitten food, and lots of good advice and reassurance. The tiny kittens were not yet heavy enough to spring the trap, so we first got them used to going in there for their food. With the weatherman forecasting an Arctic Blast, we were convinced they would die of hypothermia or get eaten by a fox, so for a few days we were on a 24/7 kitten watch.

One night I went out at 11.30 pm to check the trap and was thrilled to see two little faces looking up at the torchlight. We had caught two of them. I rang Margaret and she drove through the night to collect them, taking them home to her warm kitchen where she raises orphaned kittens in special enclosures. The next morning we caught the other two, and Margaret came once again. She told us that the first two were curled up by the Rayburn, and the future now looked bright for Minnie's four lovely kittens. They had survived, and now they would learn to be friendly domestic cats, spayed, immunised, wormed and ready to go out to kind homes.

A heartfelt thank you to angels like Margaret and the Cats Protection League for the wonderful work they are doing.

QUIZ
LITERARY FIGURES AND THEIR PETS

Can you match the famous literary figures to their pets?

1. Which female author captured wild mice and rodents – before then dissecting them?
a. Beatrix Potter
b. Virginia Woolf
c. Emily Brontë

2. Which poet was famed for having a tame bear as a pet?
a. William Blake
b. John Dryden
c. Lord Byron

3. Which literary saint kept sparrows, hiding them away in an attic?
a. St. Anthony of Padua
b. St. Therese of Lisieux
c. St. Joan of Arc

4. Which Victorian novelist had a feathery friend as their devoted companion?
a. Elizabeth Gaskell
b. Charles Dickens
c. Bram Stoker

5. Which Pre-Raphaelite started a craze for keeping a wombat as a pet?
a. Dante Gabriel Rossetti
b. Thomas Woolner
c. William Michael Rossetti

6. Name the poet who enjoyed keeping a hairy eight-legged friend as a pet.
a. Charles Baudelaire
b. Edgar Allan Poe
c. Samuel Taylor Coleridge

7. Which American author had a pet crow named Silverspot?
a. Mark Twain
b. Willa Cather
c. Ernest Thompson Seton

ANSWERS

Answers

1. Beatrix Potter

The famed children's author used to catch mice and other rodents which she kept in cages in her Lake District home. Whilst they were still alive, she would draw them in minute detail, before then dissecting them and studying their muscle structure, thus ensuring that her illustrations were as accurate as they could be.

2. Lord Byron

Byron kept a tame bear in his college room whilst at Cambridge – a way of avoiding the university's restrictions forbidding pet dogs from being kept. He could often be seen walking the bear around the grounds.

3. St. Therese of Lisieux

The young saint kept garden-caught sparrows in her attic hideaway. After being cloistered away at the age of only fifteen, Therese would look upon the birds as a metaphor for her own life. Her autobiography, *Story of a Soul*, has sold millions of copies worldwide.

4. Charles Dickens

Dickens was well-known for keeping a pet raven called Grip the Knowing – who even appeared as a character in his novel *Barnaby Rudge*. You can still see Grip today; his arsenic-embalmed body can be found in the Philadelphia Public Library.

5. Dante Gabriel Rossetti

Just one of many animals that he kept, Rossetti's wombat 'Top' was his prized possession. He soon started a craze amongst his contemporaries for wombats as pets, after regularly bringing Top to the dinner table and allowing him to sleep in the large centrepiece during meals.

6. Charles Baudelaire

Symbolist poet Charles Baudelaire kept a tarantula in a jar on his window ledge. A creepy surprise for any visitors to his home!

7. Ernest Thompson Seton

The American author of *Wild Animals I Have Known* was so enamoured with his crow Silverspot that he declared him a genius. His feathered friend loved shiny things and often raided the nests of smaller birds. 'But we must not judge him for that,' wrote Seton, 'as it is just what we ourselves do to the hens in the barnyard.'